Marc Kuhn

For information, e-mail author at info@marckuhn.com

ISBN-13: 978-1490906737
ISBN-10: 1490906738

Cover design by Damonza.com

Book website, including contact information available at:
www.deadletterbook.com

Publisher
Marc L. Kuhn
Plantation, Florida USA

For my parents, Edward and Lois Kuhn, who generously gifted me many wonderful childhood memories, including those from two summers along the Corsica River just off the Chesapeake Bay.

CHAPTER 1

Sandra Henderson was her usual attentive self as she sat in trigonometry class and attempted to keep up with Mr. Kaufman's triangular configurations drawn on the blackboard. She was not aware that the button on her blouse, the second one down from the top, had come unfastened.

Robert Harris, who sat at the desk next to Sandra, was also attentive this afternoon. He had noticed the opening in Sandra's blouse and he was attempting to strategically place his head in such a position that it appeared as though he were paying attention to Mr. Kaufman, while still allowing him to stretch his eyes to the farthest possible position to the side of his face so that he could focus on the more interesting exhibit to his right.

"Mr. Harris, can you tell the class how to calculate angle 'C' of this triangle?" Mr. Kaufman asked in a voice considerably raised above his normal volume. Robert was totally startled upon hearing his name. In fact, that was actually all he did hear as he frantically readjusted his posture.

"Ah, excuse me. What was the question again, sir?" Robert asked his teacher.

"Mr. Harris, I suggest you get your mind and eyes off the spherical aspects of geometry and back onto the angular pursuits of trigonometry. That is, after all, what I am attempting to teach you in this brief amount of time you and I have together this semester."

The class laughed. No one had any idea what Mr. Kaufman was talking about, but it totally caught Robert Harris off guard in a most hilarious way.

At that very moment, the bell rang and the students sprang to their feet in unison. It was the last class of the day. They made their exit with corresponding haste. Consequently, in the matter of the five or so seconds the bell was ringing, the incident was over and Robert was spared any further embarrassment. In this same span of time, Sandra noticed her unfastened button and hastily corrected the situation.

Centreville High School was a two-story, colonial brick building on Chesterfield Avenue in the small town of Centreville, Maryland. In 1943, just about every young person between the ages of 14 and 17 who was white and who lived in and around Centreville attended Centreville High. There was a separate high school for blacks. As in many states, segregation in Maryland schools would remain the norm for another eleven years until the United States Supreme Court ruled on the Topeka, Kansas case of Brown v. Board of Education.

America was three years into World War II in 1943, but student concerns at Centreville High School were more focused on school work, the daily responsibilities expected to be fulfilled at home, and an exploding curiosity with schoolmates of the opposite sex.

True, the boys did spend some time thinking about the war. Most who were in the lower grades, however, thought it would be over and done with by the time they graduated. The boys in the senior class had a different perspective. They knew that, come graduation in June, most of them would be enlisting in one of the armed services or waiting to be drafted. Having come from strong patriotic, rural stock, the boys were eager to join the fight. For many, the war was an exciting alternative to wasting away on Maryland's Eastern Shore harvesting tomatoes year after year or hauling bushel baskets of crabs and oysters out of the Chesapeake Bay.

The Eastern Shore of Maryland is a land mass that expands well beyond the lapping waters of the Chesapeake on the west and the Atlantic Ocean on the east. It is a sizable peninsula extending 180 miles down from its Pennsylvania border on the north, to Virginia's Eastern Shore on the south. A large wedge is cut from its eastern half by the state of Delaware. Otherwise, Maryland's Eastern Shore spans 100 miles at its waistline. Its shoreline runs twice that length.

The plantation called Chesterfield once occupied the land on which the town of Centreville was originally established and named in the late 1700s. It was selected as the county seat for Queen Anne's County because of its central location, hence its name.

Several miles to the east, tiny trickles of water with names like Mill Stream Branch and Three Bridges Branch seemingly surface out of nowhere. These meander westward through Centreville, swelling as they go and eventually feeding into and supplying the Corsica River. At the other end of the Corsica, about five more miles west, the river broadens as it empties into the Chester River which then swoops southward and dumps into the great Chesapeake Bay. Here, in the 1940s, a bountiful supply of seafood, coupled with the skills of seasoned watermen, kept packing houses busy along Centreville's riverfront. Times were improving. An aggressive poultry industry in the southern reaches of the Eastern Shore had kept much of the area faring better than many communities elsewhere that suffered through the depression.

Agriculture, however, was the main enterprise. Farms stretched outward from Centreville into the rich soils of the historic Eastern Shore. Here, family farms produced a hefty harvest of tomatoes that supplied local canneries from midsummer to well into fall. Crops of wheat and cob corn for feed occupied many of the remaining acres. Most farms, too, tended cattle and hogs, and barnyard hens along with ducks and turkeys. The labor was intense and the hours long. Everyone in the family had responsibilities. All in all, Centreville was a vibrant area and its people resilient.

The Eastern Shore was blessed with a strong heritage and its people had deep respect for the beauty and the bounty its environment provided.

Sandra Henderson and Robert Harris were typical representatives of Centreville's younger generation. Robert's family had owned the Harris Farm for as far back as the family could be traced. It was located about two miles east of Centreville. Sandra's parents were the proprietors of the town's largest hardware store, *Centreville Hardware*. It was a major operation providing both hardware and feed supplies to area farmers.

Lumber was about the only product Centreville Hardware chose not to stock, mostly because of the Fox Lumber Yard just down the road. The two businesses complemented each other well and their owners had become good friends. With all the farms in the area, both operations had more than enough orders to keep them busy and their bank accounts robust.

Sandra and Robert had daily household chores to do, plus weekend hours to devote to their family's business. Sandra helped out in the store and Robert had learned how to operate a tractor and plow fields. He was also adept at handling a pitchfork and tending to the smaller animals in the barnyard.

Both children were hard working, kept their grades up at school and were well known and liked by just about everyone in town. And in town, by the way, it was not unusual that most everyone knew everyone else. If you were a youngster you had to keep your behavior on guard. Most anything you did that may have been considered questionable was usually known to your parents by the time you arrived back home.

It was no accident that Robert sat next to Sandra in trigonometry class. Unlike the other teachers who insisted on an alphabetical seating chart, Mr. Kaufman didn't care. As the students entered his classroom back on the first day he told them they could sit anywhere they wanted as long as they kept that seat permanently. One of the younger and more likable teachers at Centreville High, Mr. Kaufman was a *pretty hep cat* according to most of the students.

George McCaffrey had already taken the seat next to Sandra when Robert came in and learned about Mr. Kaufman's innovative seating arrangement. Robert quickly approached George, subtly slipped him a buck and told him to *skedaddle*.

"That was easy," Robert thought. George, on the other hand, had no idea that Robert would have readily paid much more to have the seat next to Sandra.

Today, for a brief moment only seconds in length, his investment paid off. Robert would never forget the day he peered into the spectacular wonderland beyond Sandra Henderson's second button.

The Centreville Post
April 7, 1943
    Raymond W. Monroe, 19, son of Mr. and Mrs. George F. Monroe of Centreville, was killed in action aboard the Navy cruiser, USS Salt Lake City when it came under fire from enemy Japanese ships off the Komandorski Islands in the North Pacific Ocean on March 27th.
    There will be a memorial service at St. John's Episcopal Church of Centreville on Sunday, April 11th at 6:30pm.

CHAPTER 2

Robert Harris and Sandra Henderson had known each other for as long as they could remember. Even at a very young age, Sandra was not an unusual sight at her father's hardware store where Robert's father bought all his supplies. Robert and Sandra were the same age and grew up attending the same schools and sharing the same classes. It was not until the first year of high school that the two began noticing each other in a somewhat different way. Suddenly, Robert was more willing to accompany his father on trips to the hardware store. And too, getting up for school each morning seemed easier than it once was. Robert now looked forward to class each day. He was not necessarily enthralled by his studies as much as he was eager just to be in the same room with Sandra Henderson.

The two teenagers had much in common. They had a strong work ethic and willingly helped out at home. They were exceptionally bright. Concepts came easily to them and each exhibited a creative mind. Their maturity surpassed their age.

Like many children raised along the waterways that feed the vast Chesapeake Bay, Robert and Sandra loved being on the water. Each, at a young age, had learned to swim and handle a small boat. They were as familiar with the winding pathways of the Corsica River as they were with the streets of Centreville.

Sandra was well aware of Robert's early interest in her. She futilely attempted to control the blushing reaction she had every time he said something to her. As their relationship deepened, her emotional response evolved from flirtation into infatuation. If there was such a thing as puppy love, Robert and Sandra were well past that stage by twelfth grade. Their feelings toward each other had matured considerably. They knew, as everyone else did, the two of them were deep in the throes of young love. They were, indeed, the perfect couple, at least as perfect a couple as two seventeen-year-olds could be.

Sandra was a princess out of a fairytale. She had beautiful, flowing blond hair, radiant blue eyes and a magnetic personality. She was prom queen material, a straight-A student and president of the class. Despite all her achievements and natural allure, Sandra was still my-gosh humble and considered herself just part of the crowd.

Robert, on the other hand, was not the star athlete or

wonder boy at school, but he was enough of a catch that any of the girls at Centreville High would have been eager to claim him. A sturdy six feet tall, he was super smart and handsome, with piercing dark eyes. His name was elaborately featured in doodles and scribblings in many of the girls' notebooks. He had a quick wit and an even quicker temper. The latter seemed to be his only flaw, and one that would get him into trouble every now and then.

Along with their usual model behavior, Robert and Sandra exhibited a corresponding respect for their elders and an unusually mature sense of responsibility. These characteristics seemed to bind the two even closer to each other. And, it was these same traits that had kept their passion in check, not an easy accomplishment when you are seventeen and deeply in love.

"These are good kids," their parents acknowledged. They felt blessed to be free from some of the strife they would hear about in other families. But Robert's parents knew, too, that the war would soon come to their doorstep and peace and harmony might well be taken from them.

While Robert was an only child, Sandra had a sister two years younger. Her name was Louise. Like her older sister, Louise was attractive and popular. The two of them were close and the older they grew, the more they were able to share both clothes and personal stories.

Louise was more assertive than Sandra and less forgiving if things didn't go her way. Sandra, conversely, assumed the more passive role and would usually acquiesce to Louise. Given Louise's tendency to take, coupled with Sandra's willingness to give, the two suited each other nicely and there was seldom any rivalry or bickering, at least none that outsiders were aware of.

While Robert was an only-child, his cousin joined the family early on. Edward, or *Eddie* as everyone called him, was the son of Robert's Uncle Tim on his father's side. Eddie's mother had died when he was young. Two years after Eddie was born she ran into complications attempting to deliver a second child. Neither mother nor baby survived.

Eddie's father owned and skippered a *deadrise*, a common fishing vessel on the Bay. Dredging or tonging for oysters, and then offloading them at the packing house, made for a long and exhausting day.

Since Eddie was without a mother, his father thought it was better for his son to spend most of his time on his brother's farm. There, he would have some sense of family and, perhaps, a "brother" in Robert. So, at a young age, Eddie was welcomed into Robert's family as one of them.

Robert seldom went anywhere or did anything without Eddie by his side. Even though they were the same age, Eddie looked up to Robert as if he were his big brother. Lately, though, with the intensifying relationship between Robert and Sandra, Eddie found his presence was more awkward and unwelcome. There was an ever-loosening slack in the tether that previously held him taut to Robert. Eddie knew he had to stand aside even if it meant sacrificing one of the only secure relationships in his life. This all the more inspired Eddie's sense of independence that was intensifying within him. Other than his relationship with Robert, Eddie was pretty much a loner.

He had no real friends and took no initiative to make any. Now, as his eighteenth birthday was approaching, he began to formulate a new direction to his future...one that pointed somewhere other than Centreville, Maryland.

Life was still pretty much self-contained on Maryland's Eastern Shore during the 1940s. It had been that way for a good century and a half as its population grew. With a rich farming environment and the proximity of the Chesapeake Bay, the nation's largest estuary, the region was practically self-reliant. It was not interested in moving at a fast pace nor welcoming outside developers who would destroy the tranquil, almost colonial atmosphere. If outsiders had difficulty penetrating the Eastern Shore, its residents, likewise, found it just as difficult to find a way out.

Baltimore and Washington were near, but not easy to get to. The Chesapeake Bay was a formidable barrier. Limited roadways and an even more restrictive water ferry system provided the most plausible, but not very practical, escape. Meanwhile, family blood ran deep on the Eastern Shore. One generation after another was raised and groomed to appreciate everything the land and water provided. There was little want for much else. As a result, folks on the Eastern Shore pretty much stayed put. It just felt right.

There were some who lived there, however, who had a crab claw under their seat and it was pinching them to get up and get out. Robert Harris, like his cousin Eddie, was one of them. He yearned to explore. He wanted to see New York, California and, yes, maybe even other countries. His favorite subjects in school were geography and history. His text books teased him constantly and drove his aspirations toward one day leaving Centreville and starting a whole new life elsewhere. Sandra, of course, would be at his side.

In 1943, a new, efficient way out of Centreville had developed for a young man soon to reach his 18th birthday. Eddie had discovered it, as would Robert. Whether he went to it, or waited for it to call him, Robert knew that his days in Centreville were numbered. The war provided the perfect excuse to leave home and it was one that his father could not stand in the way of. The only obstacle was Sandra. The thought of leaving her, even knowing he would return for her later, wrenched Robert's heart.

CHAPTER 3

Now that they were nearing graduation, it was expected that Sandra and Robert would be assuming more responsibilities at home. This was the normal process that the young members of a family fell into on the Eastern Shore. This pattern played out generation after generation. College was rarely pursued.

Most children would follow in the footsteps of their parents. They would get a basic "book education" at school while learning family ethics at home and in church. Upon graduation from high school, they would join the family trade, whatever that may be. For Sandra it was hardware. For Robert it was farming.

By now, each had learned much about their family's business. More intense training was the norm for weekends. Parents felt a need to fully entrench their children into the business culture when school was no longer going to be a part of their lives. It was a way of life that was critical, parents believed, to the family's survival. It reinforced the need they had for locking their children into the environment and ensuring that the family would continue to be in well-trained hands when the elder members relinquished control.

Robert and Sandra had little time to spend alone with each other these days in the spring of 1943. School was still a part of their weekday schedule, at least for a few more weeks. Weekends, meanwhile, were consumed with absorbing the family business. Time alone was cherished and always hastily arranged for.

On one Saturday, however, their parents allowed them some slack. Robert and Sandra were free in the afternoon and they planned to go crabbing, an activity that seemed inbred in the soul of everyone who lived along the Chesapeake Bay. Maryland blue crabs were plentiful in the spring. A few bushels would keep a good number of family and friends around the dinner table well into the evening hours; a raucous ritual that included the continuous smashing of crab shells with wooden mallets along with the sharing of oft-repeated stories and jokes. With each retelling, the stories grew more intense and dramatic and the jokes more hilarious.

As soon as Robert had finished cleaning out the barn, he showered, put on a fresh shirt and clean pants and headed into town in his ancient Chevy pickup. His father had long ago stored the relic in a shed until Robert was old enough to drive it. It rode like hell and looked even worse, but Robert couldn't care less. To him and Sandra, the old truck was a golden chariot that took them to places far away from everyday and everyone.

Sandra was ready, waiting for Robert on the front porch of her home, just a short walk off the main stretch where the family hardware store was bustling with weekend business. She was picture perfect for an afternoon on the river. Her hair was pulled back in a perky ponytail and she wore a bright navy blue pair of shorts with a bib top. The straps were attached on the front with large white buttons and ran over her shoulders then crossed in the back before embracing two more large white buttons along the back waist. Sandra had no doubt made the attire herself on her mother's fancy Singer sewing machine. She wore a crisp cotton white blouse underneath. She was sitting in a rocker, her bare feet propped up on the porch rail just at the right angle to display her freshly painted red toenails. Upon seeing her, Robert felt she could have simply stayed there, frozen in time, and he could have stared at her for hours and never cared about going crabbing.

"So whatcha doin' there, boy?" Sandra jokingly said to him as he walked up the porch steps.

"Oh, I just thought I'd stop by and see if you might be fix'n for some adventure on this beautiful sunny spring day," Robert responded, as he handed Sandra a bunch of spring daisies he had picked just before leaving home. He was forever picking fresh flowers for her. A small bouquet had become a standard accompaniment to his visits.

"Well, I might be up for that see'n how you brought me these lovely flowers. What kind of adventure did you have in mind there, sonny?"

"Not to be bragging about my status in life, young lady, but I am sure you will be thrilled upon stepping aboard my fine yacht that sits moored at the city wharf waiting for us to arrive," Robert said while rocking back and forth on his heels attempting to look country humble. Sandra popped up out of the porch rocker.

"I'll just be a moment taking care of these lovely flowers and then we can be off lest one of the parents comes up with a last-minute chore that must be done or the world will most certainly come to an end."

Robert got back in the truck, started the engine then leaned over and opened the door on the other side for Sandra. Then he waved to Sandra's sister, Louise, who was peering out from the living room window as she often did when he and Sandra were in range of her pesky little sister curiosity. Robert didn't mind, however. Louise was like a younger Sandra, so how could he be angry with her? Soon, Sandra hopped into the truck, slammed the door shut and in no time the two of them were bouncing and rattling their way to the city wharf in Robert's rusty chariot. Louise was left standing on the porch, dejected and wishing oh so much that she could have tagged along with them.

Uncle Tim was a seasoned waterman who had worked the Chesapeake Bay all his life, as did his father and his grandfather. He kept the Lady J, his 30-foot deadrise, tied up at the city wharf most of the time when he wasn't oyster tonging further south in the Bay. Eddie and Robert worked the boat in the summer, especially in crabbing season. Tied up close by the Lady J was Uncle Tim's small skiff that he often let Eddie and Robert use as long as they returned it clean and in good order. Uncle Tim had the transom altered so it could accommodate a small outboard engine. That would be the very old, cantankerous Evinrude motor that started only when it wanted to. Robert seemed to have acquired a magic touch for adjusting the fuel mix and the choke at just the right amounts. No, he never had the motor start on the first try, far from it. But he never failed to get it started faster than anyone else, even Uncle Tim.

At the wharf, Robert and Sandra unloaded a few empty bushel baskets, a pole net and some line from the back of the truck and tossed them into the skiff. As Robert set about prepping the Evinrude, Sandra walked the half block down the wharf to the poultry plant. There she would ply her flirtatious wiles to persuade one of the workers to wrap up a few free chicken necks she and Robert could use as crab bait. As Robert never failed to get the Evinrude started, Sandra never failed to retrieve enough chicken necks for the day's outing.

Robert had the motor purring in no time. Sandra was taking longer than usual. He stepped up on the wharf and started walking toward the poultry plant. He suddenly hastened his pace. He saw Sandra down on the wharf being confronted by two men. She tried to pass to their right and they blocked her; then to her left and they blocked her again. As he got in hearing range Robert realized both of the men were drunk and taunting Sandra. He slowed a bit, just to silence his footsteps. When he reached them, he thrust his foot with all his strength into the lower spine of the one man. He sank to the boards below. In a flash Robert grabbed the other man by the belt and scruff of his collar, lifted him as if he were a sack of feed and threw him off the wharf and into the river. The second man, meanwhile, had gotten up and was coming at Robert. He swung but his drunken state caused him to miss horribly. Robert did not. His fist caved in the entire side of the man's face. He dropped to his knees. Robert grabbed him as he did the first man and heaved him into the river. It was not deep enough there to worry about their drowning. In fact, each man was left sitting in about a foot of muddy water wondering what had just happened to them.

Robert said absolutely nothing. He reached over and grabbed Sandra by the arm and the two of them walked back to the skiff.

"You know, you have to watch your temper," she told him. "They were drunk. I think all you had to do was say something and they would have left." Robert stopped dead in his tracks.

"Are you crazy?" he yelled. "Did you hear what that guy said to you? Hey, I thought I was pretty good at holding my temper. I threw them in the river instead of hitting them some more. And weren't you proud of me this time that I said absolutely nothing? I kept my trap shut."

"I just thought maybe a little calmer approach may have worked just as well," Sandra responded, "but I have to admit for a damsel in distress, my knight certainly can take care of things."

While it had begun with the ugly incident on the wharf, it was clearly a beautiful spring day to be on the Corsica. The trees along the banks were budding with fresh, light green leaves; dogwoods further up on the embankments spread their graceful limbs, painting the landscape with delicate whites and pinks.

And the blue crabs? Well, you could almost sense the rumbling of their back fins and legs as they scattered along the muddy riverbed.

The Evinrude puttered with a steady rhythm as Robert steered the boat westward, looking for the Alder Branch that fed into the river just opposite the long sandbar that reached out from the opposing shore. Once in the Alder, he cut the motor back to an idle and the skiff silently sliced through the calm water as Robert searched for a very specific clump of trees that reached out over the banks.

They did not have far to go. Robert turned the skiff hard to starboard, rounded the trees and aimed the bow at his target. Here, secluded just a few yards in, peering out from the shoreline marsh of tall grass and cattails, a small abandoned boatshed and adjacent dock welcomed them in.

Robert cut the motor in perfect time as the boat's bow drifted to the dock's edge. Sandra, having seamanship skills as good as any Chesapeake native, effortlessly leaped up onto the dock with bowline in hand and pulled the boat farther in until it came to rest fully inside the shed. Here she tied the line to a cleat and stood by to take the crabbing gear as Robert handed it up from the boat.

This was their private escape, an old rustic boatshed, long ago forgotten and left to waste away like so many others tucked in little alcoves along the Corsica River. The surrounding dock was still sturdy despite some rotted planks and a dislodged bollard here and there. The shed itself was in remarkable condition. Its sideboards came only two-thirds of the way down so water rot was kept at a minimum. It had once been painted a bright red and looked to have been well maintained most of its life.

Robert and Sandra would come here as often as they could. They referred to the boatshed as their *castle*. It was their sanctuary. Here they could be themselves and say and do whatever they wanted. If you were two 17-year-old teenagers in love and living in Centreville on the Eastern Shore of Maryland, this old boatshed, this castle, would be your oasis.

Robert and Sandra would not have too much time at their castle today. It was already afternoon and they had promised to bring crabs home by nightfall. Robert tied the chicken necks onto the ends of several lengths of heavy string. As he finished each one, Sandra would take it to the end of the dock, set the baited end down into the water and tie it off. When all the bait lines were set, there was nothing to do but sit quietly and wait. This time of year it did not take long before one line, then another, would show movement and soon pull away from the dock. Crabs were nibbling the chicken at the other end. Robert would take a taut line and very slowly pull it up out of the water. His fingers would pinch the line gently, one hand over the other, until the faint vision of the crab appeared as it held tightly onto the chicken with its claws. Sandra would ever so slowly sink the pole net into the water down and under the crab. At just the right moment, she would pull hard on the pole, raising the net out of the water and capturing the crab. This artful task was taught at an early age along the waterways of the Eastern Shore and few children failed to master it. Likewise, few crabs failed to escape it.

It took only about an hour for Robert and Sandra to fill two baskets with squirming blue crabs. It was time to go. They untied the bait lines, donated the leftover chicken necks to the crabs below, allowing them to eat and live another day. With all the gear back inside the skiff, they swished their hands in the water and dried them with a towel.   Before Robert started the motor and Sandra uncleated the lines, there was a customary session that lasted a few minutes. It was the one moment together the young couple naturally looked forward to when they came to the boatshed. Here they were alone, safe and free. The opportunity for an intimate time alone was not to be missed. These moments did, however, test all the discipline ingrained within each of them.   Their bodies and their emotions always wanted to extend the limits beyond the boundaries; boundaries well established for what was proper and expected from a young man and a young lady in 1943 on the Eastern Shore of Maryland. Somehow, and always at a certain point, Robert and Sandra became conscious of their parents' presence even though each one of them was busy doing other things miles down the river.

"These are good kids," their parents would say, never realizing how truthful their words really were.

CHAPTER 4

Robert rattled down Chesterfield Avenue in his truck, on his way to the city wharf to deliver a package to his Uncle Tim.

He knew it was an engine part his uncle had ordered and was in a hurry to get. Uncle Tim had it delivered to Robert's house so it didn't get left and lost on the wharf somewhere.

When Robert got to Uncle Tim's boat, he was nowhere in sight. That wasn't unusual, especially since he did not know Robert was coming. So, Robert lifted the engine cover and left the box with the part down on the ledge next to the engine. He knew his uncle would see it there when he continued working on the engine.

It was another typically glorious spring evening on the Corsica River. There was still a good hour before sunset and Robert could not resist the temptation. He left a note for Uncle Tim that he was taking the skiff out and would be back shortly. Then he got into the skiff and performed his magic on the Evinrude. He had it purring in no time. He uncleated the bowline, gave a gentle shove against the dock to push the skiff out into the open and then engaged the gear and puttered away from the wharf and out into the Corsica.

What a paradox, Robert thought. He had spent a lot of time lately contemplating ways to escape the Eastern Shore. He wanted so badly to see what lay beyond the familiar horizon that held his vision in check all his life. Then, on the other hand, when he was out on the river on a beautiful spring evening like this one, he could think of no other place he would rather be.

So much of the river, along with the land spreading upward from its shores, was still pristine and untouched by modern development. There were a few stately mansions on some scenic hillsides and other luxury homes that sat hidden and nestled within the trees. But much of the landscape itself appeared just as it had for generations before him.

Robert would often imagine pirate ships anchored off the main channel in the secret coves that lie hushed and hidden along the shoreline. Only the pirates knew where these clandestine pockets were and how to navigate them. All along the Corsica and down into the Chester River and the great Chesapeake beyond were hundreds of years of history lapping the water's edge. There had to be generations of boys just like him who trolled the waterways and envisioned adventures of high seas and great ships. It was a playland for all to cherish, no matter how old you were or how many times you had been there.

If you were a young man who had grown up on the Eastern Shore, regardless of whether you lived on a farm or over a storefront in town, the Chesapeake Bay and all its tributaries enveloped your entire being. For Robert, the Corsica River made him whole; it gave him what was his real sense of home. It embraced him with its beauty and bountiful life. On the river, he always felt carefree and secure.

Robert turned the skiff around and slowly headed back toward the city wharf. Even a moment on the river on a night like this was like hours of peaceful solitude. It left him melancholy and totally at ease.

He turned off the engine, hiked the prop up out of the water and wrapped the bow line around the usual cleat. Then he jumped up onto the wharf and stood quietly, double checking to make sure the skiff was secure. Then he tested the slack in the lines on Uncle Tim's boat to make sure they were adjusted properly for the morning tide. He knew Uncle Tim would have done this, but he felt compelled to check them. As he started down the wharf toward his truck, a nightmare began unfolding before him.

Two men came quietly up behind him. Another was approaching from the front. It was dark by now and he wasn't quite sure what was happening. But, suddenly, the men behind him grabbed him tight and held him as the third man began punching him relentlessly in the stomach, then in his face.

"Doesn't feel so good when you're on the other end, does it hotshot?" the one man said. It was then that Robert realized two of the men were the ones he threw off the wharf when they were taunting Sandra. He struggled to free himself, but they were too strong and, this time, too sober. He took a good beating until finally one of the men said "enough." They threw him off the wharf into the shallow water below and then left.

Robert felt the water soak his face, but he was disoriented. He could have been in ten feet of water and not just two and would have never known the difference. He panicked for a second or two, trying to get his bearing until he realized he was on his knees and only his legs and his face were submerged. He sprang his head out of the water and gasped for a breath. Blood drooled down his shirt and he could not see out of one eye. He was in bad shape. He struggled to climb back up onto the wharf. Once there he tried to get up. Instead, he collapsed onto the wood planks, hitting his forehead heavily onto a cleat as if it were a finishing touch to the horrible beating he had just endured. Robert would lie there, in and out of consciousness, until hours later when Uncle Tim came looking for him. His parents had sounded the alarm, worried why their always-reliable son hadn't returned home.

Centreville had a small infirmary to take care of bumps and bruises and maybe even a broken bone here and there. Big-time injuries were transported to the county hospital. That was where Robert was taken. He had some really impressive bruises all over his upper body, especially on his face. He definitely had a broken rib or two. His left eye was swollen shut. A few stitches closed the cut just above it.

Luckily, his nose wasn't broken and he didn't lose any teeth. He was treated, bandaged up and released.

His father and Uncle Tim helped him into the bed of his father's pickup. Tim jumped in beside him and wedged him in with his body. The ride home would be a little bumpy, causing Robert to mumble a few words he usually left unsaid when parents were around.

"I guess Sandra was right," Robert said between bumps and groans on the way home.

"Right about what?" Uncle Tim asked.

"Well two of those guys were the ones I picked up and threw into the river when they were bothering Sandra. They were both drunk. Sandra said I let my temper get the best of me. She said I could have probably just talked them down and they would have gone away."

"Well," Uncle Tim said, shrugging, "this ain't the first time your temper has left you huggin' the floor."

The truck delivered its banged-up and dented package to the front porch of the house, turning it over to a frantic mother who would eventually nurse it back to its original state over the next few days.

Sandra was there the next morning, sitting in a chair next to Robert's bed a good hour or more before he woke up. She simply stared at him. He was a mess. She'd tear up and begin to cry. Then, she'd stare at his battered face some more and begin to laugh uncontrollably. It was when she was laughing that Robert woke up.

"What in the world is so—ooooooh," he groaned in mid-sentence—"funny?" he asked Sandra.

"You are, Robert. My shining knight who forgot to

wear his armor when the foes came back to get even."

"Next time, remind me to take my sword, too," he responded as he groaned once more when he realized laughing with broken ribs was no laughing matter.

Robert would be on the mend for several more days. Sandra, whom by now he addressed as *Nurse Sandra*, was at his bedside every free hour she had. She was there in the morning to help him with breakfast before she had to run off to school. Then she was there with his homework for the rest of the evening until she was expected home.

Robert had to admit he liked the attention he was getting. He could not have asked for a more beautiful and caring nurse. He even thought it was worth—check that: *almost worth*—the pain.

CHAPTER 5

Eddie Harris walked into the Centreville Hardware store and made a beeline for the pretty young girl who was unpacking a carton of paint brushes and hanging them neatly on a display rack. It was Saturday morning and this is where he knew he would find Sandra, busy helping out at the family store.

"Hey, Sandra, you plan on doing some painting today?" Eddie asked.

"Nope. Can't risk getting paint in my hair," she said. "As long as these brushes don't have wet paint on them, I don't mind putting them on the rack. What's up Eddie? What brings you in here today?" Eddie leaned over a little closer to Sandra so he wouldn't be heard by anyone else.

"I need some help from you again," he said. "It's about, ah...well, it's about a girl. You gotta help me."

"Well, I have to finish this display. Give me ten more minutes, then meet me on the stoop out back of the store and we can talk. I don't have too long, though. My dad gave me a long list of things I have to get done today."

"Okay, see you in ten," Eddie told her.

Eddie was always a bit shy and he didn't share much of anything personal with anybody. Robert was the closest thing to a friend he had, but Eddie even had problems talking to Robert about certain things. Sandra, however, was different. Even he didn't know exactly why, but he found Sandra very easy to talk to about almost anything. She had become sort of like a sister to him. She never talked down to him or made fun of anything he said. The important thing, though, was Eddie had complete trust in Sandra. He knew she would never discuss anything he told her with anyone else. So, it was not unusual that Eddie would come seeking Sandra's advice anytime he ran into a personal dilemma.

Out back of the store was what was commonly referred to as *the stoop*. But it really wasn't that. Actually it was more like a large open platform or porch. It's where delivery trucks unloaded their goods and where anyone who wanted a breath of fresh air would come and sit. There were three chairs along the back wall. This morning, Eddie sat in one, waiting for Sandra's arrival. He didn't wait long. Out she came and sat down in the chair next to him.

"So you got girl problems, huh?" Sandra asked with a big smile on her face. "Well, the best girl problem solver in Centreville is now holding session right here in the very chair next to yours. It can't get any better than that. Okay, let's get to work. Is it a catastrophe?"

"Well, sort of," Eddie responded. This one girl I sit next to in history class told me that this other girl who sits another row over was hoping I would ask her to the senior dance."

"See, didn't I tell you if you combed your hair more and looked a little less disheveled the girls would be fighting over you? Just like I said, huh?" Sandra asked him with an I-told-you-so attitude.

"I'm not so sure there are girls fighting over me, but this one I guess wants me to take her to the dance and I'd sure like to, but there's this problem," Eddie said.

"I don't see any problem, except I want to check out what you're going to wear so you don't look like a farm boy bumpkin!" Sandra said. "So what problem could there be?"

"I don't know how to dance," Eddie confessed.

"Let me see you tap your foot, like this," Sandra told him as she began tapping her foot on the floor. Eddie looked down and tapped his foot likewise.

"See, if you can do that, you can dance. You just have to learn where each foot is supposed to be when it's time for it to be there. I can teach you that," Sandra assured him.

"Can you? You can teach me to dance? Nothing fancy, just some basic stuff so I don't look like a fool?" Eddie asked her.

"Sure can. After just a couple of lessons you'll be jitterbugging all over the place. We can practice in the storeroom. I'll bring a phonograph with some records and we can meet after school next week. How's that sound?"

"It sounds great, Sandra. "I knew you'd know what to

do. You just have to promise you won't laugh at me." Eddie said.

"Eddie, you know I'd never laugh at you...unless you said or did something funny!"

"Yeah, but Robert will," Eddie said.

"Well, for now this will be just between you and me. Robert will just think I'm working at the store for my Dad. Then, after he sees you're a real hot-footer on the dance floor you can tell him, so I can brag about what a good teacher I am. You know I don't like keeping secrets from Robert, okay?" Sandra explained to Eddie.

"That's a deal!" Eddie responded.

Sandra was actually looking forward to teaching Eddie how to dance. Robert wasn't much of a dancer. She and Louise danced all the time. They kept up with the latest steps and had all the big swing band records that were played on the radio. But having a boy to dance with was a lot better than your baby sister...if the boy could learn to dance, she thought.

So, after school for the next few days, Eddie and Sandra met in the storeroom in the back of the hardware store. It was just as its name said—a storeroom full of shelves full of hardware stock and supplies. But, there was a good open space in the center just the right size for dance lessons.

Pretty soon, Sandra's father was growing tired of hearing Benny Goodman playing *Bugle Call Rag*, though he did notice that some of the help in store were stepping a bit more lively. "Hmmm," he thought, "maybe I should have Sandra teach all the store clerks how to dance."

Eddie was intimidated by it all. The jitterbug was faster

than he was used to moving, let alone in some coordinated fashion. There was this other problem, too. He was not accustomed to holding a young lady around the waist and then having her move around in so...well, in so...let's just say there were some things about learning how to dance that he didn't mind practicing. In about four lessons Eddie actually looked as though he knew half of what he was doing, which was far ahead of how most other boys his age looked on the dance floor. Sandra, indeed, was a good teacher.

"I think you are just about ready to ask Margaret to the dance," she told Eddie. Margaret was the girl who sat in the other row over who was getting a little tired of sitting there waiting for Eddie to make the trip across the classroom to ask her to the dance.

"There's just one more thing you have to learn," Sandra told him.

"What's that?" Eddie asked. "What to do when I don't catch Margaret and she falls and breaks her leg?"

"Now now, you're not going to drop anybody, but you do have to learn more than just the jitterbug. There is something known as a slow dance, you know." Sandra said. Eddie took a step back and gulped.

"I thought if I was good enough at the fast stuff I could maybe get away with sitting out the slow ones," he told Sandra.

"Nice try, but I think once you learn to slow dance you'll be asking the band to play *Moonlight Serenade* until the moon don't shine," Sandra told him jokingly.

Teaching Eddie to slow dance took a little doing since

he was very hands-off at first. He couldn't bring *himself* to bring *herself* closer to him. But after two lessons, the gap between Eddie and Sandra had closed considerably and neither he nor The Mondernaires, who sang *Moonlight Serenade*, were none the worse...until an unexpected visitor showed up.

Robert walked into the hardware store and spotted Sandra's father behind the front counter.

"Hi Mr. Henderson," he said. "I stopped by the house and Mrs. Henderson said Sandra was here."

"Yeah, she's in the storeroom with Eddie. Go on back, Robert," Mr. Henderson told him.

"With Eddie? What's he doing here?" Robert half-mumbled to himself. He walked back to the storeroom and opened the door. There were Sandra and Eddie, embraced in a Fox Trot while Glenn Miller played in the background.

"Well, what the heck is all this about?" Robert said, his face already turning rash red.

"Oh, now Robert, you keep that temper of yours in check," Sandra said, walking over to him at the doorway. "I've been teaching Eddie how to dance, that's all. He wants to ask a girl to the senior dance but he didn't know how to dance so he asked me to teach him. Eddie promised to tell you as soon as he felt he was good enough so you wouldn't laugh at him—which you and I know is exactly what you would do. So put down all your huff and puff and come on in because you could use a few dance lessons yourself."

"I'd best be going," Eddie said. "I'm sorry, Robert. You know I wanted to ask Margaret to the dance, but I didn't want anyone knowing I couldn't dance. We weren't doing anything wrong, honest, just learning to dance."

Eddie thanked Sandra and made a quick exit. He'd seen Robert's temper many times and didn't want to stick around any longer. Sandra, meanwhile, seemed to have defused the situation since Robert grabbed her around the waist and the two of them began dancing ever so slowly and ever so closely around the storeroom floor.

"I think maybe there are a few steps I can teach you," he told Sandra.

CHAPTER 6

When Robert arrived home after school Tuesday afternoon, he didn't go into the house right away. Instead, he put his books down on the porch and sat down in one of several old white wicker chairs that had been on the porch as long as he could remember. It was a bittersweet week. Graduation ceremonies would be held on Friday. He was no different from any other high school student. This was a great time to be alive. No more school and nothing but adulthood straight ahead. He and Eddie would both be celebrating their 18th birthday within weeks. Robert had persuaded Eddie to go with him to the Marine recruiting office in Centreville and enlist. Both boys felt it was their patriotic duty. Underlying this motivation, however, was their mutual urge to escape the Eastern Shore and see what

35

life was really like in the world beyond. The fact that he would find himself fighting in actual combat with enemy soldiers did not faze Robert. Death was just not part of his thinking. It wasn't on his agenda. He was now a young man, soon to be 18 and invincible...so he thought. Eddie, on the other hand, was just sort of going along with Robert's enthusiasm, though his was at a much lower level.

While Robert's excitement about graduating and embarking on a whole new direction in life had pretty much consumed him by now, there was a major stumbling block ahead...and that was Sandra. He loved her very much. But he knew he would have to leave her for a while. There was never a doubt in his mind that he would return to get her as soon as his military obligation was over. As much thought as he had given all this, he had shared none of it with Sandra. He was afraid to tell her of his plans. Tonight, he had decided, it was time to do just that.

"Robert, is that you?" he heard his mother call from inside the house.

"Yeah Ma, I'm just sitting on the porch for a bit."

"There's a letter come for you today. Looks like Sandra's usual. It's on the table. And don't forget you promised your father you'd fix that gate hinge when you got home," his mother reminded him.

"Okay, I'll be there in a minute and take care of the hinge too," he yelled back to her.

The letter would be from Sandra. It was not unusual that he would get a letter in the mail from her. He would get at least one a week. He never got mail from anyone else. While they saw each other practically every day,

Sandra took delight in sending him little love notes through the mail. Then too, sometimes she would leave them in his jacket pocket or on the seat of his truck. They were not very long, nor did they rarely have anything substantive to say, not that "I Love You!" was not a critical piece of information. Robert loved getting mail from Sandra. The letters were another example of what he called her "Sandraness" and he would keep every one of them in a shoebox in his closet.

Robert picked up his books and went inside. He stopped off at the refrigerator for the customary rummage for something to eat after school. Then, he changed his clothes and went out back and down the path to the barn where he had a gate hinge to repair. All the while he kept rehearsing what he would say to Sandra; how he would break the news that he would be gone by this time next month.

Sandra was just a little surprised that Robert had told her he would stop by later that night to see her. Visits on a school night were not normal. But, of course, this was the last week of school forever and most everything considered normal was disintegrating quickly. A whole new set of "normals" was about to commence.

At a few minutes past 7 o'clock, Sandra came out onto the front porch. She knew Robert was arriving. It was hard not to notice. The old Chevy truck would belch and spit its way up the slight grade to her house. She, no doubt along with everyone else in earshot, was well accustomed to the sound of Robert's arrival.

He got out of the truck. He did not clutch the usual

handful of daisies. In the glimpse of a second the thought occurred to Sandra that this was odd. Robert always brought daisies. Oh well, maybe he was in a hurry. They kissed briefly and he took her by the hand.

"Let's go for a walk," he told her.

"Mom, Robert and I are going for a walk. We won't be far," she yelled back through the screen door.

"Okay, have a nice walk," was her mother's response.

Robert and Sandra stepped off the porch and headed down the street toward a small, somewhat secluded area where there were park benches among a clump of shade trees. They came here often since it was just down the street from Sandra's house and it was a nice place where they could sit alone and have a private conversation.

"So where are my daisies, you brute?" she asked as they sat on a bench.

"I know...I'm sorry. I had other things on my mind."

"Sounds serious. What's the matter, Robert?"

"It's about my plans after we graduate and I turn 18."

"You're leaving. I know," Sandra confessed.

"How do you know? I haven't said anything ever!"

"I'm afraid Eddie spilled the beans."

"Damn, can't that kid ever butt out?" Robert said, somewhat exasperated.

"Oh, don't blame Eddie. We were just talking last week and he didn't mean to tell me. He did say he was planning on enlisting and he inadvertently included you as the conversation went on."

"So you've known for a week? Why didn't you say anything?"

"I know you. I knew you would tell me in good time. Besides, it gave me a few days to adjust to it. Believe me, I totally understand and I think it is a wonderful thing that you and Eddie are doing for our country. But you must promise promise promise you will come back home as soon as possible because my fanny will be aching awful from sitting so long on that porch rocker waiting for you."

Robert looked her in the eyes and fiddled with a lock of her hair that had cascaded down the side of her face and onto her shoulder.

"You must now write me more than ever," he told her. "If you don't, I will think you have forgotten about me and some clam tonger set his sights on you and stole you away forever." Sandra looked up at Robert, tears slowly streaking the fresh makeup she had put on only a short while ago.

"I will write to you every day Robert Harris," she told him, "and don't you ever, ever think for even one moment that anyone else could ever have my heart."

The two sat for awhile more on the bench by the trees, holding hands and silently wondering what the future would hold and how they would accept it.

*****

Graduation ceremonies went smoothly and all the pomp and circumstance that was anticipated went off without a hitch. The speeches all were poignant, mostly about the state of war and how Centreville and its residents would do their duty. Students beamed with excitement. Parents cried with pride.

By now, it was common news what most of the graduates would be doing in short time. The girls would be homebound for the most part, continuing their family tutelage and courting their beaus, at least those who would be there to court. Most of the boys had heeded the call and planned to enlist in one of the armed services. There were already arguments about which branch of service was best. Given the way of life along Maryland's Eastern Shore, the U.S. Navy was the service of choice. Robert and Eddie, however, felt they were better suited to become Marines; well, at least Robert did and Eddie usually followed his lead.

Graduation ceremonies were early in the day, followed by a grand picnic on the school grounds. Parents contributed all the food and just about everyone in town, whether related to a graduate or not, came to eat it. It was an annual food feast everyone looked forward to each year.

Robert and Sandra were solidly glued together by this time. They wanted to take advantage of every second they had left before Robert would depart. Louise, too, had kept herself especially close by, to the point of annoying her older sister.

"Hey," Louise responded when Sandra hinted she should slack off a bit, "Robert is my big brother and I want to be around him, too, before he runs off to be some big war hero." Sandra was tiring of her sister's persistence. She was convinced Louise had a little sister's big crush on Robert even though she would never admit it.

While Sandra was growing tired of Louise's presence anytime Robert was around, Robert was growing less tolerant of Eddie always running to Sandra anytime he needed to talk about some crisis he was going through. Robert had really laid into him over the dance lessons, not because he objected to Sandra teaching Eddie how to dance, but because Eddie failed to follow through—he never asked the girl to the dance. He told Robert he lost the nerve to ask her and just decided he'd blow the whole thing off. Robert was furious with Eddie. Sandra felt badly for him.

Other than Sandra and his shadowing Robert all his life, Eddie had no one else he was close to. He did not mind; he valued his independence. None of the other kids he knew had lost their mother at such a young age. This seemed to make Eddie feel different about himself, and more alone. And now that he had enlisted in the Marines, he was not entirely sure that was the best alternative for him, but for the time being it was one that offered escape.

CHAPTER 7

Robert and Eddie were a week away from completing their enlistment processing into the United States Marine Corps. Each boy had celebrated his 18th birthday and had signed on at the Marine recruiting station in Centreville. Between high school graduation and now, they had spent a few weeks crewing on Uncle Tim's boat earning some extra money.

Every possible minute he was free, Robert spent with Sandra. The two of them had resigned themselves to the situation and were putting up a good front. Inside, Sandra was devastated knowing that soon she would be saying goodbye to Robert and she may never see him again. Robert was growing a bit apprehensive himself and was now hoping he had made the right decision. Eddie, meanwhile, showed little emotion one way or the other. He attempted to make light of the situation and often made jokes about being in the Marines. Both boys were nervous. There is no need to discuss how the parents felt. The worry raging within them was not unlike that of all parents across the nation who were now reading daily obituaries of the sons who had been killed in places they could not easily locate on a globe or whose names they could not properly pronounce.

Robert and Sandra were able to have one more trip to their castle. There would be no crabbing this time. They both just wanted to have a nice day alone on the river, the one place each would cherish most in their memories of each other.

It was overcast when they left the city wharf and motored out onto the Corsica. It was not an unusual day on the water for July, in that there was a good chance for a summer thunderstorm in the afternoon. By the time they reached the boatshed and tied off the skiff, the skies had already darkened and it had begun to drizzle lightly. They did not care. In fact, they liked a rainy day. They sat on the platform just inside the shed, away from the rain, and ate a lunch that Sandra had packed for them. Nothing much was being said. Much was being felt. Each knew this could well be their last moment alone together...forever. Sandra broke the silence.

"When I was a little girl, my father took me out on the river one day to go crabbing. He was still trying to teach me how to use the net without scaring off the crab. I was little and the pole was so long it was hard for me to handle. At first, my father was patient with me, but after losing a good five or six crabs, I could tell he was not happy. He was getting more and more impatient and that was only making me more and more anxious. Then, he started pulling up this humongous jimmy. It was the biggest crab that we had ever seen come up out of the river. He leaned over and whispered to me that if I missed it he'd leave me in the river and go home without me. I thought he was serious and I was so scared he'd actually do that. When he got the crab up to the right height, I put the pole in the water and guided it down under. I prayed, I actually prayed. Then I snapped the pole up but not quick enough. The crab was spooked and let go of the bait and started back down. I chased it with the net, trying to make one last miserable attempt to catch him. I reached too far and lost my balance. Into the river I went. Even though I was a good swimmer like all kids on the river, my father panicked. He stood up and started yelling at me. The next thing I know, he dives into the water and scoops me up in his arms. I am crying hysterically. I was panicking because I had let go of the net and I was worried it would sink. He's holding me tight."

"It's okay baby, it's okay. You're all right. You're safe. Daddy's got you," he kept saying over and over. I was clinging to him for dear life even though I didn't have to. And then, I stopped crying and slowly I began laughing. Then Daddy began laughing. Then he grabbed me at my hip and shoulder and heaved me high into the air so I would come down and belly-flop into the water. He would tell that story about fifty times for the next year or so and each time the crab got bigger and bigger." Robert laughed along with the story and tried to permanently capture in his mind the vision of Sandra's sparkling smile and the sound of her laughter.

"No wonder you became the best netter I've ever seen on the river," he told her. "Your father scared it into you. Maybe someday you and I will catch that big old jimmy and take it home to him as a trophy."

There was a sudden burst of thunder that shook the dock. The rain began coming down harder. The drops peppered the water's surface and the leaves in the trees thrashed about in the wind. By now the rain was blowing into the open end of the boatshed where they were sitting and the two of them could not escape getting wet. They didn't care.

"When Eddie and I were young," Robert began telling Sandra, "we would skinny dip in the river and on a day like this when it rained hard we'd take off naked chasing each other all along the shoreline, in and out of the coves. For some reason, with the rain pouring down and us being naked and running to beat all hell, it was a wonderful feeling of just being as free as one could ever be."

They both sat silently gazing out onto the Alder Branch, the rain pelting their legs as they dangled them over the side of the dock.

"Let's do it!" Sandra said.

"What?"

"Let's do it. You and me. Run naked in the rain." While Robert and Sandra had had many passionate moments together and there had been touching and sometimes a button or a zipper undone, they had never

45

seen each other naked.

"Well, I'm not sure--" Robert began to say. But before he could gulp out the next syllable, Sandra was up and unbuttoning her blouse. Then her shorts. Then she unhooked her bra and dropped her panties.

"See you in the woods," she told him and then she jumped off the dock and took off running. Robert practically fell off the dock trying to catch up while stripping off his clothes. He had never seen a real live girl totally naked. She had never seen a boy, except in drawings in a text book she once saw at the library.

Robert was tall and muscular with a tight waist and sturdy, long legs. Sandra was slender with a beautiful figure and a waist so small Robert thought he could place both hands on her hips and touch his finger tips together. They tried not to stare at each other...tried not to. It was an incredibly magical moment while each absorbed the exhilarating feelings that by now had consumed every one of their sensations.

The two chased one another through the marsh in the pouring rain, up and down the woods along the shore line and then into the river where they swam out several yards. Then, they swam near to each other, then nearer, then nearer. Their bodies touched. It was a sensation unlike any they had ever experienced. The years of love they had nurtured for each other and the raging emotions within them exploded beyond all comprehension. This was so new to them, so spectacularly strange and exciting. This was like never before. They were no longer high school boyfriend and girlfriend. They were adults now, just about married. Robert was going off to war. After all these years of their being together as a couple so deeply in love what more could people expect from them? They seized each other tightly and made a silent binding decision that on this wonderful rainy, rainy day in the Alder Branch of the Corsica River on the Eastern Shore of Maryland they would at last finalize their love for each other.

A good hour later, exhausted and emotionally drained, Robert and Sandra walked along the shore, holding each other's hands as they headed back to the boatshed. There, they dressed and then held each other for what seemed forever.

"I got an idea," Robert said as he dropped into the skiff and rummaged into his duffle and pulled out a knife.

"Let's leave a mark behind commemorating this moment for all to see," he said. "Let's pick a tree. Back there, that big Sassafras." He grabbed Sandra by the hand and they stepped over some rocks to a large Sassafras tree that rose tall on the backside of the boatshed. Robert began cutting into the bark: "RH+SH – 7-24-43." It took him some time to carve the message deep. He wanted it to be there forever.

"Done!" he said, "Now, when we return to this spot when I get home, this will remind us about how wonderful this day was." They slowly made their way back to the skiff and out onto the river. Robert kept taking in every minute detail, especially Sandra's face. He wanted to make sure he would remember everything about this place, this day and the beautiful girl he would come home to.

CHAPTER 8

Robert had not gotten any sleep at all. Morning had come too quickly. Today, he and Eddie were scheduled to leave Centreville and begin their military service in the United States Marine Corps. Robert was packed and ready to go. That was easy since he was instructed to bring very little. Clothes, after all, would be provided. His bag was by the front door.

His father would drive him and Eddie into town and drop them off at the recruiting office where they, along with other local boys, would be bused around the long loop north of the Bay then back down south again to Baltimore. Along the way there would be stops to pick up other recruits. In Baltimore, they would board a train for basic training at Parris Island in South Carolina.

It was still dark outside when Robert's father poked his head in the doorway to Robert's room.

"Good morning, son. Ready to go?"

"About as ready as I'll ever be I guess," responded Robert.

"Where's Eddie? He's not in his room," his father asked. "Wasn't he out with you last night?"

"He told me he was going to spend the night with Uncle Tim and he'd meet us in town in the morning." Robert explained. "But I'm a little worried about him. He told he was very nervous about the whole thing and not to worry if he chickened out at the last minute. I spent a long time trying to convince him that was not the right thing to do."

"Oh I don't know," his father said. "I suppose it is kind of hard to finally realize you are leaving home for the first time. Not everyone can be as strong as you are. I'm sure he'll show up when we get there. You still have time so you might want to grab something to eat. No telling how long it'll be before you get something on the road."

Robert was finishing up making his bed. He would leave the room neat before he left, making sure everything was put away. This room had been his own for as far back as his memory went. He took one last look around, sighed and walked out the doorway.

"I'm not hungry. I have some cookies in my bag and an apple. We may as well get started so you can get back. I know you have things to do," Robert told his father.

"Okay, I'll see you in the truck in a minute," his father said. He noticed that Robert was even not quite himself this morning. He was exceptionally quiet and he looked tired and dr awn. He figured his son was going through a tough morning. After all, like his cousin, Robert was leaving home for the first time, too, and probably winding up on the other side of the world trying to stay alive. That, his father thought, would probably make anyone not quite himself at the moment.

As he stepped out the front door, Robert's mother was standing at the bottom of the steps in front of his father's truck. She was a mess. Tears flowed freely down her cheeks and she held a dish towel, wringing it nervously in her hands.

Robert came down the steps, put his bag down and wrapped both arms around his mother. She sobbed uncontrollably.

"It's alright, Mom. It's time for me to go. I'll be back in no time and I'll have lots of stories to tell you," he told her. "Take care of Dad, okay?" His mother could barely talk.

"I love you, son. You take care of yourself and be safe." she told him.

"I will, Mom." Robert relaxed his arms, gave her a squeeze on the upper arm and kissed her on the cheek. Then he picked up his bag and got into the truck.

The ride into town was mostly silent.

"You sure you are feeling all right, Robert?" his father asked. "You're sweating."

"Yeah. I'm just tired and a little anxious."

"Did you get the letter that was left for you on the porch chair last night?"

"Yeah, I got it." Robert reached into his pants pocket and pulled out a now crumpled letter. He rotated the envelope, flipping it between his fingers. He was in deep thought. This letter was different from the usual ones he was used to getting. This one was disturbing. His father detected a small tear forming in the corner of his son's eye. Then, it slowly slid down along the side of his face. Robert was quick to wipe it away.

"I know it's tough," his father said, "but your mother and I are very proud of your decision. This is a great country we live in and it is up to us to keep it that way. You are a good son and we love you. Just remember that always and know that we'll be here thinking about you all the time."

"I know, Dad, thanks."

"And we'll keep pestering Sandra just so she knows she is not alone in missing you," his father assured him. "I know she will keep those letters coming to you, that's for sure. That girl loves to write you letters."

The truck pulled up to the parking spaces in front of the recruiting office. Robert put the letter back in his pocket, grabbed his bag and got out of the truck. His father, meanwhile, met him at the curb.

"You go on back, Dad. This could take a while waiting for everyone to get here."

"I don't see Eddie," his father said.

"Since when is Eddie ever on time?" Robert asked him. "I'll tell him you said goodbye and that I chased you off."

His father started to put out his hand, then simply got closer and embraced Robert with both arms.

"Be safe, son. Be smart. That will get you through it all. Try to write as much as possible so we know you're okay."

"Goodbye, Dad." They looked each other in the eye for a moment, then Robert stepped up on the curb and went into the recruiting office. His father got back in the truck and slowly backed out of the parking space and headed down the road.

It would be another hour before a small bus drove up, stopped and hissed in front of the recruiting office. By now there were a dozen or more young men standing out front. Each one had a small bag in his hand and a blank stare on his face. At the recruiting officer's coaxing, they all arranged themselves in a single line and stood alongside the bus. Eddie was not among them. The recruiting officer shrugged when no one answered "here" as he called out Eddie's name when roll was taken.

"You know where he is?" he asked Robert since they had signed up together and had the same address.

"No," Robert answered nervously.

"There's always one we gotta chase down. What else is new?" the recruiter said. "Okay, everyone on the bus."

The line of boys slowly disappeared into the bus. The driver was finishing up cleaning the windshield with a damp rag which he then tossed under his seat as he got in the bus. He pulled the door lever shut and started the engine.

The bus backed out, then noisily shifted gears and began its way down the street. On its way, it passed right in front of Centreville Hardware. Just inside, peering out between the signs posted on the storefront window, Sandra Henderson stood and watched the bus go by. Her eyes swelled with tears as she gently raised her arm and waved the palm of her hand ever so slightly.

Robert was gone.

*****

By early afternoon there was a knock on the front door of the Harris farmhouse. Mrs. Harris came to see who it was.

"Hello ma'am, I'm the Marine Recruiter here in Centreville. I saw your son, Robert, off this morning. Fine boy you have there. He will make a fine Marine. You will be proud." the recruiter told her.

"Thank you," Robert's mother responded. "But why are you here?"

"I'm looking for Edward Harris, ma'am. He was a no-show at the bus this morning. Do you know where he is?"

"My goodness, no," Mrs. Harris said. "I have no idea. I can't believe he didn't go. It's all we've talked about for the past month. I do hope nothing's happened to him. Did you talk to his father?"

"That's not your husband, correct, ma'am?" the recruiter asked.

"No. Eddie's father is Tim Harris, my husband's brother. You can find him down on the city wharf. He has a fishing boat there named the Lady J."

"Okay, I'll go there," the recruiter told her.

"Eddie's not in trouble is he?" Mrs. Harris asked.

"Well, he's officially sworn in and he officially did not show up when and where he was supposed to, so that makes him officially AWOL, if you must know the truth. But it happens a lot. Some boys get jumpy at the last minute. Just scared, that's all. We find them, slap them on the butt and put 'em on the next bus, that's all. You see

Eddie, tell him to come see me right away." The recruiter got back in his car and left.

In a few minutes he pulled up at the city wharf and parked the car. The Lady J didn't go out this day. Her engine had developed a miss and Uncle Tim wanted to find out why and fix it. Any good waterman on the Chesapeake did not leave things to chance. If the engine was making some kind of noise it was telling you something. If you ignored it, you'd no doubt find yourself stuck in the middle of the bay with no power and begging for help. Not a good situation to be in, especially if the weather turned bad. And, if you were stuck powerless in the middle of the bay that is exactly when the weather would turn bad.

The Marine recruiter walked up to Tim's boat and knocked on the stern. Tim was butt-out, the rest of him buried deep into the opening where the engine was mounted. He crawled out and looked up at the Marine.

"Can I help you?" he asked.

"Mr. Harris?" the recruiter asked

"Yep, that's me, but I'm a little too old to be off fighting the Japs," Tim responded.

"It's your son, Edward, sir. He didn't show this morning when the bus came to pick up the boys. Do you know where he is?"

"Why no," Tim responded. He stood up now and came toward the stern of the boat.

"He was with his cousin. He told me they were going to go together. I said my goodbyes to him yesterday."

"Well, that didn't happen. Robert showed up on time but Edward didn't. I think he may have gotten the willies at the last minute and took off. It happens," the recruiter explained. Tim was worried.

"Well, I know he was a bit nervous and he told me he was having some second thoughts, but I didn't think he'd take off. That's not like Eddie. You can usually count on him when he says he's going to do something. What happens now? Is he in a lot of trouble?"

The recruiter took his cap off and scratched his head.

"The longer he's gone, the more trouble he's in. If we can find him quick, we can maybe work things out as long as he gets on the next bus. But for now he's officially AWOL. If you see him, tell him to haul butt and find me, faster the better."

"Okay, I'll do that. He's a good boy; lost his mother when he was young. She died. Sometimes that shows up in him every now and then. I hope you take that into consideration."

"Well, just make sure he comes to me if you find him." The recruiter put his hat back on and walked back up the wharf to his car.

By early evening just about everyone in Centreville knew that Eddie Harris was AWOL. Sandra was saddened by the news that he was missing. She was not surprised that Eddie may have, as she put it, "got the heebie jeebies" at the last minute, but she felt terribly sorry for him. She knew Eddie well. He had shared a lot of his feelings with her. His mother's death had had a huge impact on him. He pretty much kept that to himself, but he had discussed it often with Sandra. He trusted her and Sandra had never broken that trust. She hoped he would decide to come to her soon since he was in trouble and probably knew it. In the past, when Eddie had a problem, the first person he would go to was Sandra. She knew that Eddie was sorry he had signed up with the Marines, but Robert could be intimidating. Eddie thought he'd be better off in the Navy where he'd blend in more easily. But if he had, indeed, decided to go AWOL at the last minute, she hoped for the best and that wherever he went he'd find peace of mind. Knowing him as well as she did, Sandra did not expect to see Eddie returning to Centreville.

The Centreville Post
July 26, 1943
Russell Andrew Davenport, 20, son of Mr. and Mrs. Frederick R. Davenport of Centreville, was killed when his ship, the USS Gwin sunk after being torpedoed by Japanese destroyers in Kula Gulf, Solomon Island, on July 13th.

Memorial services will be held on Thursday, July 29th at 3:00pm at Grace United Methodist Church in Centreville.

CHAPTER 9

Not much was said on the bus ride to Baltimore. Most of the boys knew each other but this was not a time to debate sports or talk about girls. No, a good number of the boys appeared deep in thought; others had their hats pulled down over their eyes and were presumably sleeping.

Robert sat near the back of the bus. He took the letter out he had received the day before and read it again. He must have read it a dozen times since it was left on his front porch. It was as if he did not believe what he was reading so he kept reading it over to make sure it said what he thought it said. Then he just stared at it for several minutes. Eventually he folded it back up and put it in his pocket. He stared out the window for a while and ate a few of the cookies he had brought with him. He was exhausted, but could not seem to settle down, even for a short snooze on the bus.

The letter had changed everything. His earlier enthusiasm for leaving Centreville and going off to a new adventure had lost all its luster. It was as if he had been suddenly slammed by some tremendous weight and it had taken all the life out of him. He had a lot on his mind. He figured the train ride would be long and the seat more comfortable, so he planned to catch up on some sleep then.

The minute he arrived at Parris Island, Robert knew a dramatic change in his life was taking place. He decided right then that he would have to seriously put his temper in check and not react emotionally to anything that was directed at him. He had heard stories about Marine boot camp. He knew it would be hard. But he was a different person now, even though much of the change had come over him only within the past day. He was resolved to be tough and under control. He was going to use the Marines and the war to vent every negative element of energy out of his body. He was determined to abandon all former experiences and begin anew as a mean, ruthless Marine. This, he had decided, would be his new way of life. This would be his way to survive the unbelievable news he was given on a one-page letter left on his porch as he left the confines of Centreville.

Robert would spend seven weeks at training camp. There, he would do things he had never done in his life. Most of the time was consumed with weapons training and by the end of camp Robert had clearly impressed his superiors. He scored as high, if not sometimes higher, than any boot on record. He embraced the physical fitness training and his body took on a new and remarkable strength and agility. He excelled in every other area of training. When he graduated, he had accomplished his first objective and that was to rebuild his mind and his body into a whole new being. There was no question, he was as prepared for combat as anyone could be given his age and experience.

If he could have arranged for transportation, Robert had an opportunity to go home for a couple of days before he would be shipped out. Anyone else who had that chance took it gladly. It would be a welcome relief from the past seven weeks of torture. Robert turned it down. He said he had no reason to go home. He had already distanced himself from his past and, indeed, from most of his present. He had no close friends from training camp and had pretty much earned the reputation of being a loner who didn't talk much but sure read that letter he had at least once every day.

Second Division, Marines, New Zealand was Robert's destination. He was actually excited. He'd be ship-bound for quite a while and he would be traveling half way around the world. The farther from Centreville, he thought, the better. He had no idea exactly where he was going and what he would be doing after arriving there. The answers to all those questions were simply a matter of taking orders and following them. At this, Robert excelled.

In 1943, competition for real estate in the Pacific Ocean was at a critical stage. The Japanese were dug in on islands and atolls scattered across the waters between their homeland and the south, central Pacific. The allies, by now, had a clear list of objectives that were essential to defeating the Empire of Japan.

One such objective was the Marianas, a chain of islands 1500 miles south of Japan. Taking the Marianas from the Japanese would reward the United States with a strategic base practically in the enemy's backyard. From there the Americans could launch air strikes throughout the mid-Pacific and north. But if the Americans wanted the Marianas, they would first have to take Betio on the western side of the Tarawa atoll in the Gilbert Islands. This would provide a necessary land base to support the attack on the Marianas.

Securing Tarawa under the Stars and Stripes would involve a battle that lasted some 76 hours and killed almost 6,000 Japanese and American troops. The prize? A strip of land about two miles long and less than 800 yards across at its narrowest point.

In October, 1943, the 2nd Division, U.S. Marines, was recuperating in New Zealand after its campaign in the Solomon Islands for Guadalcanal. This was the first major offensive by the Allied forces against Japan. The battle for Guadalcanal lasted a grueling six months before the Japanese gave up. Now in New Zealand, the Marines were getting a much needed rest as many of them tended to healing their wounds or recovering from malaria. It also allowed time for replenishments to arrive and take the place of those who were lost at Guadalcanal. Among these fresh recruits was Robert Charles Harris, a young Marine from a small town on the Eastern Shore of Maryland.

*****

Robert would not be in New Zealand for long. The 2ⁿᵈ Division was slated to play a major role in the assault on Betio Island within just weeks. He underwent some orientation and special training for a week and then it was back onboard another ship, the USS Doyen, an attack transport vessel.

The Doyen left Wellington, New Zealand on November 1ˢᵗ. Onboard were the Marines from the 2ⁿᵈ Division. They would join other transports participating in the operation at a small island named Efate, which was used as a staging area for the attack on Tarawa. Here the men rehearsed amphibious landings using the actual crafts they would deploy in—among them Amtraks and Higgins boats. Robert was assigned to one of the latter.

This would be one of the first assaults when these kinds of amphibious landing craft were to be used to transport troops into battle. Previously they carried only supplies and equipment. They were not heavily armed and the passenger area was unshielded, two deficiencies sorely evident when the boats would eventually approach the beach at Tarawa.

Before they left Efate, the Marines were instructed that they should consider leaving directions or any revisions to their wills at that time. Also, it would probably be the last opportunity for some time to get a letter out through the military post office. Robert had planned on writing Sandra a very specific letter for some time. He had kept putting it off but now, he supposed, would be the time to do it. It took him most of one night to write the letter. He wanted it to be precise. All military letters went through a censorship process. Letters written by the troops would have to be read and approved by the commanding officers.

While Robert knew his letter to Sandra contained no military information that would cause his CO to censor it, it did contain some personal information that he really did not want to share with anyone, especially some stranger he had known only a week. But he had no choice so he decided he would write the letter using references that only Sandra would understand. When he was done, he took the letter over to the mailbox for letters that went to the CO for approval. He held it in his hand first for a good minute before dropping it through the slot in the box.

"Okay, there it goes. Now I can die," Robert whispered under his breath.

The fleet arrived at the Gilbert Islands on November 20th. It was the largest American force yet amassed for a single assault in the Pacific. There were 17 aircraft carriers, a dozen battleships and eight cruisers. Destroyers, 66 in number, joined them as did 35 transport ships filled with Marines. Overall, 35,000 troops would be launched onto the beaches at Tarawa.

Robert leaned over the rail of the Doyen in the early morning hours. He fondly remembered seeing a large fleet of the remaining skipjacks and the more current deadrises line the Chesapeake from shore to shore during some of the opening days of oystering or crabbing seasons. That sight was nothing like the vision before him now. As far as he could see was an incredible display of American military might. Despite how nervous and scared he was about his first time in combat, he could not help but be inspired by everything he saw. He actually felt optimistic despite his pounding heart as he climbed into his launching craft and grabbed hold of a ledge on the starboard side.

Adding to the difficulty of launching an assault against some of Japan's best troops, the American effort would be hampered by miscalculations and unanticipated problems. The tide levels expected for launch time were misjudged. The Higgins boats were not able to make it over the coral reef offshore. Consequently, many sat stranded atop the hard coral, easy targets for enemy fire. A good number of them were merely blown apart where they sat. Their troops were disgorged in the explosions, flying through the air and then landing in the shallow water beneath them.

Those aboard crafts that were not yet hit, quickly abandoned them, finding themselves in chest-high water with the weight of full gear and no protection from the horrendous shower of machine gun fire from some of the 500 Japanese *pillboxes* that populated the rise above the beach.

Robert peered slightly over the side of the Higgins boat and watched in horror at what was happening all around him. There were bodies everywhere, many of them floating lifelessly in the surf. Many were in pieces only. The water had turned red all around him. Most of the Marines in the boat with him were hunched over with blank stares or quivering lips that were muttering prayers and other thoughts out loud. Many were throwing up from nerves or seasickness.

Years of riding out storms or heavy swells on the Chesapeake had made his body accustomed to rough seas. He was alert to everything going on around him. This was definitely not the Chesapeake. Nor was it the tranquil, scenic shore of the Corsica River. And, most certainly, it was not like looking down at the water lapping up against the dock of an old abandoned boatshed where he sat next to a beautiful girl whose laughter he could no longer hear. No, where he was now was unlike anything he could have ever envisioned. This was some strange, horrific nightmare he was in...and all of it was so far from home, and so distant from all that he had once known and loved.

A total of 125 landing craft, Amtraks and Higgins, were launched that day onto the beach at Tarawa. Only 35 completed their mission.

CHAPTER 10

The family and friends of Robert Harris would never get over the fact that within only months since they watched Robert walk across a raised platform and receive his high school diploma that he was now a victim of the war. This was all too soon. He had just a few months ago boarded a bus with other young men from Centreville and went off to training camp. How could he have wound up in so short a time on the other side of the world in a place no one had ever heard of and have his life end there? Yes, this was all too soon.

So much of what the people of Centreville learned about the war came from impersonal daily accounts they read in the newspapers or reports they heard on the radio from places that seemed almost imaginary. Only for those who had suffered the great loss of a loved one who had been killed in the war did it become so much more. To his family and friends, Robert Harris was someone they knew well. He was not impersonal or imagined. Now, the war had come home to them. Now, it was real. Now, they could feel its pain in their hearts.

Robert's body would not be coming home to his beloved Eastern Shore. His dog tags had been pulled from a body fragment in the shallow waters on the beach at Betio. The rest of his remains were gone.

People would have to rely on their memories; memories of a once vigorous, carefree and well liked youngster who grew up on a farm just outside Centreville, and who fell in love with the beautiful daughter of the family that owned the town hardware store. These memories would have to suffice.

Sandra Henderson, who had her whole life before her, felt anything but that. The world as she had known it was over. She, at this point in her young 18 years, had no hopes, no dreams and nothing to look forward to. The loss of Robert was beyond anything she had ever felt possible and she would, indeed, never be the same again.

1943 was a difficult year for the town of Centreville, Maryland. Too many of its young boys had gone off to war. Too many would never return home again. One young son, Edward Harris, presumed still alive, may as well have been counted among the war's dead. Believed to have gone AWOL on the eve of his departure for training camp, Eddie was never seen again.

*****

Forward and aft lines from the decks of the USS Doyen were dropped over the sides as sailors below on the dock retrieved them, and then secured them onto the huge cleats mounted on the dock's edge. The Doyen had arrived safely at the U.S. Repair Base in San Diego, California. It was returning from Pearl Harbor where it had dropped off casualties from the initial assault on Tarawa.

While in San Diego, before departing with another supply of fresh Marines for operations in the Pacific, the Doyen would undergo repairs of damage caused by enemy shore batteries and torpedo planes while engaged in the assault on Tarawa. Fortunately, the ship had suffered no casualties while under fire. Damage was confined to non-essential areas including a row of empty equipment lockers and a small portion of the ship's mailroom. Regarding the latter, mail from the 2nd Division, Marines and other personnel in New Zealand, was offloaded onto the dock at San Diego where it would then be taken to the base post office for final distribution to the recipients across the mainland.

Among the several canvas bags of mail from the Doyen was one designated "D-E-A-D L-E-T-T-E-R" across one side in red stenciled lettering. These were letters that had been sorted out because the address destination on their envelopes, along with any sender information, could not be deciphered. Included inside this bag were letters damaged while in the Doyen's mailroom when the ship took on enemy fire during the assault on Tarawa. One of these letters had been written by a Marine who came from a small town on the Eastern Shore of Maryland. It was intended for the Marine's girlfriend and contained information he wanted her to have, assuming he would not be returning home. Unfortunately, the letter's envelope had suffered considerable damage. Most of the information on it was gone, scorched or burned away entirely. It would be designated "dead" and sent to a "dead letter" facility where personnel were authorized to open and read the contents in an attempt to discover either the recipient or the sender.

Tony D'Angelo, with his trademark cigarette dangling out of one side of his mouth, recklessly drove the jeep along the waterfront of the base at San Diego, weaving in and out of sailors, crates, ship gear and other vehicles. Extending out into the water, like long slender fingers, were docks that were flanked on both sides with as many as six or more large ships. The ships' lines were pulled taut down onto the docks below where they were made fast to huge cleats. They represented just about every kind of vessel in the United States Navy; everything from a landing craft or an oil tanker, to a destroyer or an aircraft carrier.

D'Angelo's jeep screeched to a halt alongside the USS Doyen. He jumped out and walked just a few steps over to the stack of mailbags that sat on the dock. He picked each one up and tossed it into the back of the jeep.

D'Angelo then drove back down the waterfront, showing no improvement in his driving skills. After he executed a bunch of hastily made left and right turns, he pulled up to the door of a small building. Above the door was a stenciled sign that read, "Base Post Office."

D'Angelo went inside, dragging two of the mailbags, one in each hand. Just inside the door was a small outer room barely large enough for a narrow table. The room was painted a pale government green. The walls were peppered with Navy and Marine recruitment posters and various signs spelling out postal procedures.

One wall divided off the rest of the building's interior. Cut out in the middle of this wall were several small "teller windows." Here postal services and other related transactions passed in and out through a narrow opening at the bottom of each window. To the right, cut into the same wall, were two slots, one labeled "Local On-Base Mail" and the other, "All Other Outgoing Mail." At the one end of the wall was another door.

D'Angelo dragged the two mailbags across the floor and then turned around as he approached the door. He proceeded to ram his butt against the door causing it to burst open into the large back room. Here, long tables ran along the walls on two sides. Arranged in the middle of the room were several rows of "pigeonhole" shelves atop narrow support benches.

Two men stood sorting letters from bins balanced between their stomachs and the ledge of the bench that supported the shelves. A radio was turned on somewhere in the room. The faint beat of swing band music kept the sailors tapping their feet as they picked up letter after letter, looked at the address on the envelope, then scanned the pigeonholes until the right one was located, into which a letter was then jettisoned off their fingertips.

"Hey D'Angelo," yelled one of the mail clerks sorting envelopes, "it's your turn to go through the dead stuff. Have fun."

"Yeah, I know," D'Angelo yelled back as he threw a mailbag onto the stack in the corner. "And wouldn't you know it, it's a pretty full bag this time. Apparently the Doyen took a hit right in the mail bins. Lucky me, I might be here the rest of the night."

"Hey, there's probably Tarawa mail in there, don't you think?"

"Probably so," D'Angelo said, "which means more than likely there are some dead letters written by dead Marines."

The other mail clerk, whose name was Manowitz, suddenly stopped sorting the envelopes he held in his hand.

"You're right," he said. "There probably are. That makes those letters twice as important to try to figure out who's supposed to get them. I'll stay and help you, Tony, but you can't be chain smoking those cigarettes in my face all night. I'll puke with all that smoke."

"Hey Manny, I appreciate that and just 'cause you're helping me and all, I'll take the smoke outside, okay? But let's get something to eat first then we'll come back and hit the bag."

Usually, higher-ranking personnel would be delegated to open and read dead letters, but there was a war on and that meant normal procedures were subject to being "un-procedured" sometimes. This was one of those times. So, Tony D'Angelo and Sheldon "Manny" Manowitz, two mail clerks stationed at the Naval Repair Base in San Diego, were authorized to open military mail designated "dead" and attempt to identify the writer or the person to whom the letter was being sent.

By 2200 hours, D'Angelo and Manowitz had gotten through most of the mail in the dead letter bag. They sat at a table in front of three bins. One was labeled, "Dead Dead," meaning there was no useful information in the contents of the letter to determine the intended recipient or sender. These letters would be destroyed. The second bin was labeled "Resolved." These letters were each placed in a new envelope now correctly addressed to either the recipient or sender along with a form that explained the letter had been damaged and why it had been opened. The third bin was labeled, "Follow-Up." The recipient or sender for these letters was still not determined, but they contained enough information that additional investigation might lead to discovering where they should go.

Shortly before midnight, the men were finally reading the last two letters in the bag. It had been a long night but they both realized how important any one of these letters could be to a loved one, especially if the sender had lost his life.

Manowitz picked the last letter out of the bag and began his investigation. D'Angelo, meanwhile, was still working on the one he had, but he could not decide exactly what to do with it. Most of the envelope, what was left of it, was scorched. The address was almost totally destroyed. The letter "C" appeared to be the first letter of the city. There was also a "D" which may have been the last letter of the state. There was no return address anywhere on the envelope. The word "free" had been clearly written in the upper right-hand corner which signified a postage stamp was not necessary because it was military mail.

The contents of the letter intrigued D'Angelo. It was written to a girl named "Sandra" and it seemed to be from someone close, most likely a boyfriend or young husband. There was no information that helped decipher who Sandra was and where she lived, nor who wrote the letter, other than an "R" at the end. With very little else to go on, this letter would normally be declared "dead" and tossed into the bin to be destroyed. But there were several hints, almost puzzle-like, that implied the sender was giving clues to Sandra as to where to find some kind of treasure.

D'Angelo knew the letter did not warrant being placed in the "follow-up" bin—there just wasn't enough information to go on—but it piqued his curiosity enough that he did not want to declare it dead. He decided to break regs and when Manowitz wasn't looking, D'Angelo slipped the letter and its envelope into his pocket. He figured if he put it in the "dead" bin, it would be destroyed anyway. So who cared if he took it with him with the intent of studying it more on his own.

CHAPTER 11

Sandra Henderson was undergoing a change. She was no longer the bubbly ever-smiling beautiful young lady with the great sense of humor and magnetic personality. She still put in her hours at the family hardware store every day, but she had lost all enthusiasm for the work and for the customers. She simply went through the motions and nothing more. It was no secret, everyone knew she was hurting from Robert's loss. Everyone cut her slack and left her alone.

And, alone she was most of her free time. She would eat very little, have no place to go and nothing she wanted to do. She stayed in her room. There, she attempted to deal with the hurt; hurt that was now overtaking her physically. Early on, while she was attempting to deal with Robert's leaving, she has not been well. While most of her discomfort eased as time went by, she still felt weak and tired most of the time. After endless nagging from her mother, Sandra finally made an appointment and went to see the doctor.

Later in the week, Sandra awoke and got out of bed earlier than usual. She went to the kitchen where her mother was going through her daily routine of getting breakfast ready for everyone.

"My, you are up early today," her mother said as Sandra walked into the kitchen and headed straight for the coffee pot.

"Mother, I owe you and everyone else an apology," Sandra said as she spooned some sugar into her coffee, then stirred in some milk.

"And what do you have to apologize for?" her mother asked.

"I have been selfish and feeling much too sorry for myself. If Robert were here he would be angry with me. After all, he was the ultimate optimist in my life and if I am to keep his memory alive, then I must live up to what he would have expected of me. I have given this a lot of thought and today I shall stop behaving as I have and start putting the *Sandraness*—as Robert would say—back into my life. It is time for me to move on. Not away from Robert, but just move on to where he would have wanted me to be."

"Well," Sandra's mother said, "I am not sure why all of a sudden you've hit yourself over the head with a baseball bat and come to reason, but I will welcome back the old you with open arms. You've been missed." She put down the spatula in her hand and crossed around the table to where Sandra was standing.

"We have all suffered a horrible loss; you the most," Sandra's mother told her. "We all know that, and we are all here to help you get through it." The two embraced, holding each other tightly for some time, before the smell of burned toast brought them back to reality.

Sandra's father noticed the difference in his daughter's demeanor almost immediately. He decided he would not question her about it. He was just happy to see her coming back to life. She was an important part of the family, in more ways than one. Her father realized she was definitely a business asset. Her incredible personality and good looks, her intelligence and the ease with which she could handle even the most disgruntled customer—all these things had significant impact on the hardware store's financial statement. He knew well that many customers came in, sure to pick some things up now and then, but they really came in to see her. There wasn't one of them who didn't fancy that maybe one day she would be receptive to him personally and not so much to his hardware question of the day. She was a customer lure much more efficient than running advertisements in the newspaper. Her father would tell her mother that men just went nuts over her and bought bags of them with matching bolts just to have an excuse to have her wait on them.

Sandra joined the family at the dinner table that night and stayed around to help with the dishes, just as she had always done in the past. Afterwards, Louise left the house to work on a school project with one of her classmates who lived down the street. Sandra dried the last dish and added it to the stack in the cabinet above the stove. She folded the dish towel and put it on the counter next to the sink. Then she asked her mother to come to the living room where she knew her father would be sitting, sifting through the day's mail and still nursing his cup of coffee from dinner. She motioned her mother to sit next to her father and then she took a seat across from the two of them.

"I have something I want to discuss with you," she told them.

"Is this another revelation like this morning's?" her mother asked jokingly, "because I'm not sure I can take two in one day."

"Well sort of," Sandra said, "but I have to get this all out and I beg you to let me just do that and hear what I have to say. Then we can get on with whatever is to happen. Will you promise me you will let me do that?"

"Sure thing," her father said. "So get it out."

"I know you will be disappointed in me and I never had the intention of hurting you," Sandra said. Then she paused for quite some time. The room was dead silent. At first, Sandra looked down at the floor. Then, with determination, she sat up, straightened her back and looked directly at her parents.

"I'm pregnant," she told them. "Simple as that. I'm pregnant. I knew I was for some time now, but my recent visit to the doctor made it official. And, it is getting difficult to conceal it any further. It's Robert's baby. He died never even knowing. You have to understand that we were always the best kids ever; the most responsible— everything you and his parents ever wanted of us. But we failed you. And, it was only just once and on our last day together. But that was all it took. And, this is what I want to try to get you to understand. First, I have given this a lot of thought. I am not just some kid who played around with some boy. No two people were ever more in love than Robert and me. You knew that. Everyone knew that. My God, the whole town of Centreville knew that.

There was never a question that we would get married. If it hadn't been for the stupid war, you and I would probably be sitting here this very minute making plans for the wedding. So what if some priest or somebody didn't make it official? I don't care if we were not married by law. We were already married in our hearts and that's what really counts.

We were so frightened that we would never see each other again and that everything we had ever dreamed of would never come to be. And that is exactly what has happened. We thought about getting married; about running off to Elkton and just having the ceremony to make it official before he left. But we couldn't work it out without any of you wondering what was going on. So on our last day together before he left, things just got out of hand. We didn't plan it that way, absolutely not. It just happened. We didn't care anymore about what people thought. We had done our part. We were good kids. We just couldn't stop. We did not want to lose each other forever. And, just as we feared, now we have.

So, this is what I am thinking. I am thinking this was all meant to be. I mean, we were together just one time, our first time, and I get pregnant. It was meant to be. Robert was not coming back. He left me something to live for;

something that was a part of him, something that he and I would share even though he would not be here. It was meant to be. And I will not feel any shame or remorse. I have part of Robert growing inside of me and I am at peace because of it. I have something, someone, to live for. I ask your forgiveness if I have shamed you. But I also ask you to understand that I embrace this baby and I am happy that it will be with me. If I can't have Robert, then our baby is the next best thing."

There was a brief pause, a quiet moment in the room that did not last long. Sandra's mother sighed slightly and then spoke.

"I am glad you finally trusted your father and me to share the news. We've been waiting patiently," her mother said.

"What? You mean you knew?" Sandra asked. She appeared startled. "How could you know? Louise is the only one I've told and I know she wouldn't have told you."

Sandra's mother reached across and took her by the hands and held them tightly in hers.

"You were sick for several weeks a while back. Add to that, other subtle changes I've noticed, not to mention it's getting a little obvious despite your attempts to hide it with baggy clothes. It is easy for a mother to spot the symptoms of pregnancy. I went through it all twice, remember? No, you were too young to remember."

Sandra's father leaned forward.

"Your mother and I have had some time to think about it. So you can ease your worry that we are going to explode and throw you out along with the baby and don't forget the bathwater too. We won't hide the fact that we wished it hadn't happened, but we understand what you have told us and I'm not so sure either one of us would disagree with how you feel."

Sandra felt a slight sensation of relief, a lessening of some of the stress that was bottled up inside her.

"I'm not sure what to do," she told her parents. "I will work as hard as I can at the store and help out here at home. I want to stay here. I want my family to share all the good things about this and not dwell on anything negative. If you feel I have brought shame to the family, then I will move away. I'm not sure how, but I will figure it out."

"No, no. No one is throwing you out," her mother assured her. "You are our daughter and a wonderful one at that. It goes without saying that our new grandchild is welcomed here," her mother responded. "But your father and I feel that Robert's parents need to be told about all this right away. They are part of your family now. So we think that is the next step you need to take. They need to know."

Sandra said she would take care of that the next morning. Then, she laughed slightly.

"I suspect once I take one step into the baby doctor's office everybody in Centreville and everyone on the Corsica will know. You can count on that!"

CHAPTER 12

Sandra Henderson would never get over the loss of Robert Harris, but her determination to have his memory live on was evident the minute her baby was born. She would devote her life to ensure he would grow into a successful and well accomplished adult. He would, she knew, escape the boundaries of Centreville and the Eastern Shore. It was his father's goal; it would become his son's destiny and she would make sure it happened.

Sandra also decided she would thoroughly embed herself into the family business. She learned every aspect there was to know about hardware, from the names and sizes of every nail, bolt and screw to knowing how to expertly handle any tool in the store.

At first, the male customers took her newfound knowledge as a joke. A woman was the last one they wanted hardware advice from. This attitude didn't last very long, especially among the regular customers. She soon became well known all around town and the surrounding waterways. There was hardly a man who hadn't been to Centreville Hardware and maneuvered himself, sometimes in ridiculous fashion, just to have her wait on him. She had matured beautifully. And, for more than good looks, by now she had been nicknamed the *hardware lady* and that is how everyone referred to her. If you were working on a project and had a hardware question, her answer was the one you wanted. Customers would wait, puttering around in the store, until she was free and able to suggest what gauge wire to use or how to install a well pump. There was nothing in hardware that she did not know about or how to do. It had become her focus and, despite a bevy of men constantly wooing her, she showed no interest and welcomed none of them into her life. She wasn't rude about it, but the locals knew...she had loved once and never would again.

And so it went for the next several years. With her mother's help looking after her child, Sandra was able to keep her promise of working hard at the family store. Her son, Robert Harris Henderson, better known to everybody as simply, "RJ" for *Robert Junior*, brought the family much joy and once he started attending school it was obvious he had inherited his father's smarts.

*****

Sandra walked around the boat, inspecting every square inch as she went. She pulled on the fittings, tapped the fiberglass hull, crawled under the bottom and almost took a bite out of it just to see how it tasted.

"It needs a motor," Sandra said looking up at Tom Jennings, the man in the blue polo shirt with the *Jennings' Boats* logo on it.

"Yes she does, Sandra, but the boat itself is exactly what you've been telling me to look out for. This one just came in this morning and from what I can tell, it's in really good shape. The best thing," Jennings continued, "is that the buyer is desperate to sell her so you're getting a sweetheart deal. And, because it's you buying it, old friend, I'm just going to hit you for the basic fees and taxes and nothing more. I'll eat the profit just to see a smile on your face."

"That's very kind of you, Mr. Jennings," Sandra said. Then she turned to the 8-year-old boy who by now had climbed into the boat and was sitting at the helm and spinning the steering wheel.

"Well my little crabbing mate, what do you think? Is this the one?" Sandra asked him.

"Can I get to drive it, Mom?" RJ asked his mother.

"Sure thing," Sandra told him. "So, is this the one?"

"Yes, this is the one," RJ replied.

"Well then, Mr. Jennings," Sandra said as she turned to her friend, the boat dealer, "I think you just sold a boat, but there is one condition."

"What's that?" Mr. Jennings asked.

"You have to put an outboard on her and it has to be an Evinrude. I won't buy it if it doesn't have an Evinrude on it."

"Sold!" said Mr. Jennings. "I'll inspect it bow to stern and make sure everything is in perfect condition and have an Evinrude hanging off the transom by the end of the week. You can take her out this weekend."

"Did you hear that, RJ?" Sandra asked her son. "No more borrowing or renting. We're going crabbing on Saturday in our very own boat. How 'bout that!" RJ was all smiles.

"This is better than a birthday, Mom!"

The Evinrude would get a lot of hours put on it over the next several years. Sandra and RJ became fast and furious crabbing buddies. But one thing of note: Sandra bypassed the Alder Branch every time they approached it.

"How come we never go down there?" RJ asked one time.

"Oh, that just dead-ends real quick. Nothing down there but cattails and mosquitoes," his mother would tell him. But out of the side of her eye, she never failed to look down the Alder as she motored by. Always, the feelings returned; feelings she experienced many years ago when she and her boyfriend tied up at an old abandoned boatshed tucked away just around the bend, inside a small cove.

Sandra and RJ loved the Corsica River and together they would accumulate many shared and valued memories of their time spent on it. Some were simply peaceful evenings with a beautiful sunset; others featured violent summer storms that would come up with no notice and feel like the end of the world was upon them.

Mother and son would eventually be known for the stories they would tell about their adventures on the river. RJ had a collection of crab stories about the big ones that got away. Each crab grew larger with the retelling of its great escape. Sandra, meanwhile, would often tell the story of the two drunks who motored by her and RJ one afternoon. They were young men, locals no doubt, who had been out fishing, probably since sunup. They had also been drinking a lot of beer, probably since sunup. Sandra and RJ were anchored and had a few crab lines overboard when the two approached in their jon boat.

"Why lookie here, Johnny, a sexy bitch boat captain," the one man said. "Now, you don't see that every day on the river, do yuh?"

By now, the two boats were side-by-side and the one man grabbed hold of Sandra's boat.

"This could be our best catch of the day," the man named Johnny said. RJ pulled a boat hook from its clamps inside the hull and walked over and stood right across from the two men.

"You men locals?" RJ asked.

"Local enough," the other man said. "What's it to yuh?"

"Well then you no doubt heard of the hardware lady, haven't you?" asked RJ.

"Yeah, I seen her at the hardware store. She's one tough good lookin' lady. What of it?"

"Well, that one tough good lookin' lady is my mother," RJ told them. "And if you had had a few less beers you would have recognized that's her sitting at the helm. But I think I heard you refer to her in some other way that she and her young son—that's me—would take offense at."

"You're a pretty smartass kid for your age, sonny," was Johnny's response.

"It's not me you have to worry about," RJ warned. "If you know my mom's reputation then you know she can handle just about any tool you put in her hands, from a staple remover to a chainsaw...and especially that other tool that's in the cubby right next to her knee. Now, unless you would like my mom to demonstrate how that particular tool works, I suggest you take your hand off the gunnel of our vessel, drift off a foot and then put your engine in gear. Can I ask you fellows to do that and we'll wish you tight lines the rest of the day."

"Now, there's no sense in getin' all hot and angry about it. We were just sayin' hello, that's all." Nameless then let go of the gunnel of Sandra's boat, pushed off lightly and his friend, Johnny, put their engine in gear and they trolled off down the river and out of sight.

"My God," Sandra said. "You fended off two drunks without even giving me a chance to stand up. Your father would have had them both bloody and treading water. I know that because that's exactly what happened once. I can't believe you did that so easily and so bravely. I was sitting here scared to death."

"Maybe it was some part of Dad that was showing itself," RJ said. "But trust me, Mom, I was shaking like all get out inside."

"And what's with this tool in the cubby?" his mother wanted to know. "It's just a flashlight for God's sake. You made out like it was a sawed-off shotgun or somethin'."

"I know you taught me not to lie, Mom, but I thought it might make me sound more convincing than just holding a boat hook."

"You surprise me every day, RJ. I am so happy you are part of my life...the same one you just saved!"

As RJ grew older, he learned the Corsica and all the waterways linked to it as well as anybody raised on the Chesapeake. He had his father's love of the river and instinctively knew its every current and every mood. But most of all, the river had his respect.

Then, it seemed like overnight that RJ, like his father before him, was sitting in trigonometry class and taking his girlfriend crabbing on weekends, leaving his mother home alone, but with a smile on her face. And, it wasn't long before RJ was learning the hardware business, too.

*****

It is 1961 and the traditional family cycle on the Eastern Shore continued for the Henderson clan. RJ was about to graduate from high school. His aunt Louise and her husband, Hank Wheeler, were celebrating their tenth anniversary. He was a waterman who worked the local waters for oysters and crabs. Louise worked at the family hardware store, mostly watching over inventory and customer orders.

At 36, Sandra had been blessed in that she had had a lot of support as a single mother. Her mother and sister were always there when she needed help or someone to watch RJ. Her father was practically a full-time Dad to her son. Even Uncle Hank would go out of his way to take RJ with him everywhere he went. Indeed, RJ had a full family holding him up and seeing that all his needs were met, especially instilling within him a love of family. All this would never make up for not having his real father being there with him, but it was the next best thing.

One situation, however, had finally tripped the cycle this time around. It was RJ himself who caused it to happen. His work at the hardware store led to an interest in construction. During last summer's vacation he got a job with a construction company that was building a new marina nearby on the Chester River. It was then that he decided to break tradition. RJ would be the first Henderson to go off to college. He wanted to learn architecture and someday, he hoped, he would run his own development company.

As all these things unfolded over the years and RJ's future appeared secure, Sandra found herself more and more alone again. She was very proud of her accomplishment, however. She had raised Robert's son to become a fine young man—a college graduate—well liked and respected by everyone, just as his father was. But, unlike his father, RJ was a lot more even-tempered. Sandra was happy if that was the only difference.

Sandra was especially proud that her son had broken the lock the Eastern Shore held on most of its offspring, something his father wanted, but had not accomplished. She had no idea where her son would eventually wind up, but she did know that he would escape Centreville. That was for sure. RJ was well on his way to a successful career. His personal life, too, showed great promise. He had met a very bright young real estate agent to whom he found himeslf glued for the next several years with a happy marriage coming well into focus.

Sandra was quite pleased with herself. Robert would have been proud. She was so sorry that he wasn't there to be a part of it. Even after all the years that had passed, her heart had never healed. She still felt his loss as if it happened only yesterday.

CHAPTER 13

It is the summer of 1979 and Sandra just celebrated her 54th birthday. There was a nice dinner in her honor along with the usual oversized birthday cake. RJ and his family came over from Baltimore where they lived. He was 35 this year and was a vice-president with a large real estate developer with offices in Baltimore and Philadelphia. He and his wife, Pat, had two children who were spoiled rotten by Grandmother Sandra, especially when they came to stay for the weekend.

Sandra's parents were both gone by now. Her father had died in 1965 after suffering a second stroke. Her mother continued on for another ten years until she stood up after breakfast one morning only to collapse onto the kitchen floor. A massive heart attack had taken her suddenly and with no notice.

Sandra's big birthday bash was winding down. The dishes were all washed and put away. RJ and his clan had left for the ride back across the Chesapeake. Hank had missed the party. It was his busy season and he was on the lower Bay for the week. Everyone else had said goodnight and they slowly scattered in different directions homeward.

Louise and Sandra sat together on the front porch.

"I'm glad you're my sister and my best friend all these years. I hope you realize how much you mean to me. I don't say that often and I guess I really should," Sandra told Louise.

"Well, the two of us are pretty much bolted together." Louise joked. "Besides, we know too many secrets about each other that neither one dare leave the side of the other or those secrets would be all over Centreville by sunup. That'd be my guess."

"They're showing The Sound of Music on TV tonight. Want to stay and watch the VonTrapp family escape the Nazis again?" Sandra asked.

"Sure, as long as you don't sing along with all the songs," Louise said very seriously.

"Well, let's go," Sandra said as she got up out of the rocker. "I'm told the hills are alive and they won't wait for us to get comfy."

The two ladies walked into the house, and closed the screen door behind them.

*****

Sandra was comfortable now that she was well into the second half of her life. She had several accomplishments she could point to. First, RJ. He was a fine young man, well on his way to a successful life with a wonderful family and a rewarding career...and it was all happening outside of Centreville. She, on the other hand, had not wasted her life. She had turned around her misery after Robert's death into becoming a successful businesswoman who was well admired and liked by everyone around her. She was at peace with herself, though never so with the loss of Robert. She missed him terribly and never stopped thinking how horrible his life must have become after that day when she peered out from the hardware store window and watched his bus disappear down the road.

It was a beautiful sunny afternoon and Sandra had a few errands to run. There was enough help at the store that she would not be missed. So, off she went. It was no surprise that she made up an excuse to drop off some new dock line at the boat. The river, as it did for Robert, always had a magnetic pull on her. Anytime she was near, she could not avoid stopping by the boat just to check its mooring lines if nothing else.

The boat, like her, was showing its age now. The seats were faded and had developed wear marks and cracks. The bright white fiberglass hull was now dull and yellowing. The Evinrude was not as peppy as it once was and its combustible components now rebelled when she attempted to bring the engine to life. But Robert taught her well with the old Evinrude on Uncle Tim's skiff. She could always get this one started, too.

Dusk was nearing as she stepped aboard and opened a storage bin and stowed the new dock line she had bought. She sat at the helm and looked out onto the Corsica. She loved twilight. Its palette was void of vivid color and, instead, cast darkened silhouettes of the treetops against a pale yellow sky and stretched long shadows across the river's surface. She could not resist. She got the keys out of her purse, started the engine, released the lines and slowly motored out onto the river. It was quiet and peaceful. She couldn't be happier.

Within a short time she had reached the mouth of the Alder Branch. Normally, she would have passed right on by, but this time was different. This time, Sandra felt a calling. She wanted, just once more, to visit the boatshed and feel its wonder, just as she did so many times with Robert.

As the bow of the boat slowly turned to starboard, Sandra felt her pulse increasing as she entered the Alder Branch and proceeded inward. Within moments, there it appeared, the protrusion of trees extending out and over the water's edge. Beyond that and tucked inside a small cove would be the boatshed. It came to her that it had been many years since she was here. Perhaps the shed was long gone. But, as she inched the boat just beyond the outgrowth of trees, there it was, as if it had stood silently in time, unchanged and waiting for her return. True, it appeared to list slightly to one side and there were some planks missing from the dock and the pilings were not all as vertical as they once were, but it was all there, still intact and very much as she had remembered it. Her eyes began to tear up. By the time the boat nudged gently against the dock's edge inside the shed, she was sobbing uncontrollably. She turned off the engine, jumped up out of the boat and tied it off on the same cleat she had secured

Uncle Tim's skiff so many times so long ago. The sun was just about setting. She walked out onto the dock and sat with her legs dangling over. This is exactly where she and Robert sat for hours. She rubbed the rough, dried wood planks next to her. This is where Robert would be, she thought.

As she sat there, still crying, an unusual feeling came upon her. She felt happy of all things. Her tears were of joy, not sadness. The best times of her life, with the love of her life, had been here in this very spot. It should be remembered in happiness and love, she thought, and that is how she decided she would act. She was so glad she had decided to come.

She sat and relived many of the moments she remembered here. Robert would tie the chicken necks onto the long strings, then hand them one by one to her. She would take them to the end of the dock, drop the baited end down into the water and tie the other end off on a piling. She would unwrap sandwiches and snacks and spread them out on the unfolded paper on top of the dock. They would sit together and eat, still watching the crab lines for the telltale tugs.

She and Robert would sit here next to each other and hold hands and often he would wrap his arm around her and hold her tight. They would kiss. "How many times had they kissed here?" she wondered. She laughed out loud.

How surprised Robert would be, she thought, at knowing he left a child behind; a wonderful child who was so much like him and who had achieved so many of the things that he had wished for himself. RJ was the reward for their misfortune. She had completed her mission and had a sense of fulfillment and peace of mind.

The memories swirled about in Sandra's mind and each one brought a feeling of joy and sense of contentment. And then, as if with some directed purpose, her thoughts turned to the very last time she and Robert were here together. She told him how her father coerced her into learning how to net the crabs. She remembered losing her balance and falling into the water. Her father dove in after her. Robert told her how he and Eddie had skinny dipped and run naked in the pouring rain along the shore line when they were little kids. She remembered the look on Robert's face when she began taking off her clothes. She saw him stumbling down the dock trying to remove his pants as he ran after her.

She remembered all this as if it had happened only moments ago. How happy these memories made her feel. She had not felt this way since she was a young girl totally immersed in love with a young boy.

Sandra got up and stood for a very long time on the edge of the dock and stared out onto the water. Then, she looked back at the boatshed and thought how magnificent it still was. She smiled.

Ever so slowly, she began unbuttoning her blouse. She took it off and folded it neatly and placed it down onto the dock. She unhooked the back of her bra, removed it and then folded it neatly and placed it down on top of her blouse. She removed her shoes and placed them next to the folded clothes. She unbuttoned her slacks, removed them and then took off her panties. These, too, she folded neatly and placed onto the stack of clothes on the dock. She stood there for some time, naked, staring out onto the water. She never stopped smiling.

"I will love you forever, Robert Harris...forever," she whispered to herself, and then she dove off the dock and into the water.

CHAPTER 14

When she passed by the family house on her way home, Louise noticed right away that all the lights were out. It was late and Sandra would always be home by now and she would leave the porch light on all night. Louise slowed down to see if Sandra's car was farther back in the driveway. It wasn't. Louise didn't feel good about this. Her sister was the most compulsive person she knew. Sandra rarely broke routine and for her not to be home at 10 o'clock at night was definitely rare. She drove farther down the street until she reached her house. When she got inside she began calling people. She called RJ to see if he had talked with his mother. He hadn't. But he tried to ease Louise's concern.

"Maybe she went to the movies or she's out late with some people. She is a grownup lady, Aunt Louise. She is allowed to roam about as she wishes," RJ assured her. "And what if, Aunt Louise, she just maybe decided she'd finally go on a date with one of those guys who are always pestering her?"

"Okay, I'll try to settle down," Louise told him. "But if she calls you for any reason, let me know right away, okay?"

"You bet, and you do likewise just so you can tell me I was right," RJ said. They said goodbye to each other. RJ hung up the phone. He was worried. He didn't want Louise to know that, but he felt the same way she did—this was not like his mother.

Louise continued to call some other people. She spoke with the assistant manager at the hardware store. He told her that Sandra left the store mid-afternoon just after putting a new seed display in the front window. She told him she had some errands to run. He told her not to bother coming back, that there was enough staff for the night and he would close for her. Louise tried a few other people, but no one had seen Sandra.

She left the house and walked the half-block back to the family home. She went inside and looked about. No one was there. Then she left a big note taped to a side chair and moved it right in front of the door so Sandra couldn't miss seeing it. It read, "Call me when you get home—regardless of the hour! L."

Louise went through the motions of trying to stay calm. She had no one to talk to. Hank was still on the Bay and wouldn't be home for another day. She took a bath and got ready for bed. She had to get up early in the morning and put some customer orders together so they were ready to be picked up. She couldn't sleep, however, and spent most of the night watching television and fretting.

When the alarm went off, Louise shot up off the sofa where she had finally fallen asleep. She walked into the bedroom and turned off the alarm clock. She had not forgotten. She knew instantly that Sandra had not called her. Did that mean she never came home? She dressed in a hurry, skipped breakfast and left the house. Within moments, when she arrived up the street, she saw that the family house was undisturbed. Sandra had not been there at all. Louise was beside herself, almost hysterical. She called RJ again and this time he did not console her. He told her to call the police and report Sandra missing, then stay there; he was on his way.

By the time RJ arrived, the front of the house was lined with police cars. The house was a beehive of activity with police all over the place. His heart started pumping uncontrollably. He drove up on the front lawn, jammed the car into park, jumped out and ran up to the porch steps. By now, Louise had spotted him and she ran to him with her arms outstretched. Tears were streaming down her face.

"She's dead, RJ, she's dead, my God she's dead." Louise was hysterical. She fell into RJ's arms and wept endlessly. RJ didn't know what to do. He wanted to console her, but he was so shocked by the news himself he was at once an emotional wreck. The two of them held each other sobbing for the longest time. Finally, Louise's neighbor pulled her away and coaxed her to go next door with her. RJ, meanwhile, turned to the officer who was standing close by.

"Tell me what happened," he asked. The officer explained that Detective Randolph was inside the house and would go over everything with him. The officer escorted RJ inside and he and the detective sat down at the dining room table.

"First of all, I am very sorry for your loss. I knew your mother, just like everyone in town did. She was an amazing lady and you have my heart-felt condolences."

"Thank you," RJ said, "but tell me what happened."

"We are still piecing it together. We are hoping to find some clues here in the house. She apparently left the hardware store yesterday afternoon. Your sister told us to check to see if her boat was still tied up at the city wharf. It wasn't, so we assumed she was on the river somewhere. I am told this is not unusual for your mother to do. I'm told she would often go off in the boat by herself and just cruise the river or maybe go crabbing."

"That's true," RJ said, "She always told me it was her therapy. It gave her time alone to think and just enjoy the river. She loved being on the river"

"Well, I am sorry to have to give you the details. But some boys were out fishing early this morning, up the Alder Branch—you know where that is?"

"Yeah, it's not far. We never went into the Alder. My mother just told me it dead-ended and went nowhere. Is that where she was? I'm surprised she went there."

"Well, these boys spotted her in the river. She was just floating face down. She had no clothes on. They were all folded and stacked neatly on a nearby dock where her boat was tied up. It looks like she went skinny dipping of all things and something terrible happened. We don't know what. Somehow, she mysteriously drowned. Maybe the coroner will have more information later. But for now, it's just a sad, sad mystery. I am so sorry."

RJ was numb. He went out onto the front porch and sat down on the rocker, the one his mother had dibs on anytime she walked out onto the porch. Anyone seated in it instantly knew to get up and offer it to her. He had visions of her sitting in it at that very moment. He slowly rubbed the chair's arms with his fingertips knowing his mother's arms had rested on them for as long as he could remember.

RJ sat there for quite a while, trying to accept what had happened, but it was unacceptable. Tears slowly formed in his eyes one by one and then made their way out and down the side of his face. He simply did not know how to deal with it. His mother had meant everything to him. She had given up her entire life, devoting every minute of it to his well-being. He knew the only reason he had escaped the Eastern Shore was because his mother had made it her goal. Yes, it was his father's goal before that, but it was his mother who made sure it was never abandoned. This was a horrible loss that would never heal.

*****

You might have thought that Sandra Henderson was some kind of high official, like the governor of the state. The entire town of Centreville seemed to come to a complete stop when it learned of her death. Sandra would have had no idea how many people she had touched in one way or another. She was the most popular girl in high school and that reputation would continue to live on with her for the rest of her life.

RJ had driven back home to Baltimore that night to get some clothes and take care of family matters. He got up early the next morning and drove back to Centreville to begin the arduous task of preparing his mother's funeral. When he drove up to the family house he could not believe what he saw. There, spread over most of the front lawn, were flowers and a lot of other things—things being hardware materials like tools and paint cans, ropes and chains, buckets and ladders and just about anything and everything you would find in a hardware store. RJ stood silently looking at all this in disbelief. An older man, who had just added a wood saw to the pile, saw RJ and walked over to him.

"Hello Mr. Henderson. I'm Bill Peterson. You don't know me, but I've been a customer at your family's hardware ever since I moved here in the 50s. Your mother always treated me special. She was one wonderful person. She sold me that saw years ago. I wanted to get a bigger one and she insisted I didn't need a big saw to do what I wanted to do. So she talked me into buying that smaller saw. It cost less too. And, she was right; it was perfect. I thought I'd leave it here for a bit just as a show of my respect for her. I guess a lot of other guys felt the same way about stuff she had sold them. I know it must look kind of weird to you, but it's sort of a nice tribute to your mother, given that her nickname was 'hardware lady'."

"Well, Mr. Peterson, I agree, it's a little weird," RJ said, "but I think Mom would have gotten a big laugh out of it and felt touched that so many people came here thinking of her. Thank you for being one of them."

"It's still pretty early," Mr. Peterson responded. "I think this pile is going to grow once the word gets out. I have to go. I'm really sorry for your loss. Going to the hardware won't be the same anymore."

RJ thanked him and then went up the porch steps and into the house. Louise was already there spending her nervous energy going from room to room and straightening up anything that needed straightening up.

RJ stood silently and scanned the room. Any moment he expected to see his mother coming in from the kitchen or her bedroom or anywhere in the house. But she didn't. The hard reality that she was, indeed, gone, was finally beginning to sink in and it felt rotten.

"You look like you got about as much sleep last night as I did," Louise said. "Want some coffee?"

"That would be great," RJ answered. Louise went to the kitchen where she had a fresh pot on the stove and poured RJ a cup and took it back out to him in the living room.

"I guess we need to go to the funeral home first and take care of things there," RJ said.

"I hope you don't mind, but I already spoke with Mr. Collins on the phone this morning and he asked us to be there at 11," Louise told RJ.

"No, that's fine that you did that. We'll do all this together because I will need your advice on lots of things, especially clothes for Mom and stuff like that."

"She and I spent many a night talking about everything imaginable and the subject of our funerals did come up once so I have a pretty good idea of what she wanted. I do know that my father had included her when he bought the family plots way-back-when, so there is already a place for her to be buried unless you want to do something else."

"No, no. The family plot is where she belongs," RJ said. "Besides that, it's here on the Eastern Shore and I don't see her up and leaving her home now. But we have to remember to leave a small bouquet of fresh cut flowers with her like she told me my father would always bring her. She'd like that."

Louise and RJ sat there for awhile more, teary-eyed and gently swirling their spoons in their coffee. It was just all too much, and much too soon.

CHAPTER 15
1983 – Philadelphia, Pennsylvania

Donald D'Angelo drove his new Ford Tempo around the block several times hoping someone would finally pull out and give up a parking space. This was the one thing he hated most about coming to his parents' house in South Philly—trying to find a parking space. The blocks of old row homes ran one after the other, interrupted occasionally by a corner storefront, a church or a school. The D'Angelo house was in the middle of the block, but still close enough to Pat's and Gino's cheesesteak stands that the aroma of fried thin beef, onions and melted provolone cheese was a long-accepted part of the environment.

The streets here are narrow, lined on one or both sides by bumper-to-bumper parked automobiles. Most of the streets are one-way, making a repeated circular route looking for a parking space all the more difficult to navigate. Donald D'Angelo had already watched two cars pull away from the curb, but each time the car in front of him quickly maneuvered itself into the vacant slot. Not surprisingly, seasoned South Philadelphia drivers were professionals at parallel parking and had no problem maneuvering into an open space no matter how tight. In South Philly, parallel parking was a skill learned at an early age and one that easily identified native sons from outsiders who had no concept of how to move a car sideways and wedge it snugly between two others.

Donald tried to be patient. He really had no choice. Finally, his turn came. A big hulkin' baby blue Cadillac pulled out just as he was coming down the block. He was first in line. It was almost sinful, he thought, parking his compact Tempo where a Caddy El Dorado once stood— what kind of challenge was that?

He got out of the car, zipped up his jacket and walked the two blocks back to his parents' house. This was not a fun visit. He had made many like it the past few weeks. His dad, Tony, had died last month following an ugly, drawn-out bout with lung cancer at an early age. He was only 60. Like his mother, Donald had tried over and over again to get his father to quit smoking but he would have none of it.

"If cigarettes don't kill me, something else will," his father would say. "These days who knows what it'll be. They tell you all of a sudden how bad some foods are that you've been eating all your life. Jell-O will probably kill you for God's sake." That's how Tony usually responded to anyone who criticized his smoking. Then he'd always add, "And don't forget I lived through the big WW2 and if that didn't kill me, nothin' will."

Donald let himself in with the key he had and closed the door behind him.

"Ma, it's me. Where are you?" he yelled.

"I'm in the kitchen, Donny. I just made fresh coffee for you. Did you eat? I got half a hoagie here from Sal's if you want it." His mother was an endless supply of food and drink. "What can I feed you?" was permanently part of her greeting to anyone.

Donald threw his jacket on a chair and entered the kitchen.

"Yeah, I could go for a hoagie. I didn't get lunch today; too much going on with the holidays coming and all. What's funny is that there is a rush on George Orwell's *1984*. Now that it's only a few weeks away everyone who hasn't read it wants to catch up so they can laugh in the New Year." Donald took a seat at the kitchen table and his mother unrolled the white paper that wrapped the hoagie, then put the sandwich on a plate and put it down in front of him.

"I got hot peppers in the fridge. Want some?" she asked.

"Nah, not today, Ma. My stomach's not the old garbage pail it used to be. I'll take some of that coffee though. So how's it going? Make any progress?"

Donald's mother had decided to sell the house. It was too much for her to handle without Tony there to take care of it. Her sister who lived out in nearby Delaware County had invited her to come live with her. Donald was glad. He loved his mother dearly, but the thought of her moving in with him was enough to spike his blood pressure sky high. He felt guilty about not offering, but he knew it just would not work. His aunt's offer was a godsend. It took him off the hook and he knew the two sisters always enjoyed each other's company. Both had lost their husbands so they had even more in common. Hopefully it would be the perfect solution now that his dad was gone.

"I got most of the upstairs cleaned up," his mother told him. "Everything I don't want is in the back bedroom. You'll have to call the Salvation Army or Goodwill or someplace to come take all of that stuff and the furniture, too. Nothing there is worth much so I may as well donate it all and maybe someone can use it. My things that I'm taking with me are boxed up in the front room. I put my name on those boxes so you can tell they're for me."

Donald finished up the hoagie and went over to the sink to rinse his hands.

"There's one box you should go through and see if you want anything in there," his mother told him. "It's the one marked 'Navy.' It's full of stuff your father saved from when he was in the Navy during the war. I don't think there is anything worth anything in there but maybe you'll see something you want."

"Okay, I'll take a look. Anything else you need me for while I'm here?"

"No, I guess not. I just feel bad throwing out a lot of things without your father being here. He'd be going nuts and yelling at me, I know, but I miss him so much. It's just hard to keep thinking he's never coming back. I wish he hadn't been so stubborn all those years about his smoking. Maybe he'd still be here if he had just given it up."

"Well, don't beat yourself up, Ma. We all tried to get him to quit many times. He was just a cantankerous old man when it came to that." Donald was halfway up the stairs by now, on his way to the back bedroom.

There on what had become a guest bed that no one ever slept on because no guests ever came to stay overnight, was a carton with "Navy" scribbled on one side. He sat down on the bed and began going through it.

There were a few patches that his father had kept from his uniforms along with ribbons and a collection of citations he had earned. His father had not seen much action in the war. He actually lucked out by being assigned to the military post office where he was a mail clerk for a good part of his enlistment. He was stationed at the Navy base in San Diego and after that, he finished up doing some ship time, but nothing directly in any of the battle zones. Donald sifted through a stack of photographs of what he guessed were base shots of ships and some buildings. There were several pictures of sailors his father must have served with. The rest of the box contained various travel brochures from places his father had visited, along with his discharge papers and a brass belt buckle that hadn't had any *Brasso* applied to it for a good many years.

At the bottom of the box was a notebook with a rubber band wrapped around it. Donald started to take the rubber band off, but it was old and brittle and simply fell apart in his hands. He opened the notebook and inside was a singed envelope containing a letter. The envelope was half gone and much of what remained looked as though it had been in a fire. It had been stamped with red stenciled letters that read, "Dead Letter." The notebook contained pages of what appeared to be different parts of addresses. There was a page marked "postal zones" and it had three columns of numbers listed from the top of the page to the bottom. Other pages had long lists of street names on them and further in were pages of city names and small towns. There was another page with state names listed on it. Donald recognized his father's handwriting and knew all these notations were his, but he had no idea what they were about. Then, Donald carefully opened the envelope and took out the letter and read it. It was bizarre. It started out with "Dear Sandra." His mother's name was Ellen so the letter wasn't to her. He couldn't think of anyone in the family named "Sandra." Maybe his father had a girlfriend when he was in the Navy, before he had met his mother. Donald carefully folded the letter and put it back inside the envelope. He'd finish reading it when he got home. He slipped the letter into the notebook and the notebook back inside the box which he then picked up and carried downstairs.

"I'm going to take this whole Navy box with me and go through it more thoroughly later," he told his mother. She had moved to the living room where she was watching *Edge of Night* on television, one of several soap operas that were part of her daily regimen.

"Do you know anything about this notebook with all the numbers and city names in it and this letter to someone named 'Sandra'?" Donald asked.

"Shhhh," his mother hushed him. "Wait 'til the commercial."

Donald sat in the chair across from her. He knew he'd have to wait. There was no interrupting his mother's "stories." House rules. He had learned that long ago when he was a little kid living there. He patiently waited until the next commercial break. His mother then turned toward him.

"That's a letter your father brought back from when he was a mail clerk in the war. He told me it was what they called a dead letter since it was damaged and they couldn't tell who it was supposed to be sent to or who wrote it either. But it was about some treasure this young man was writing this girl about and he was giving her clues where to find it—at least that is what your father thought it was all about. He was obsessed with the letter. He'd spent a good two years trying to solve the clues or locate the place it was supposed to be mailed to. He'd go over maps and post office lists and anything else that might help him find out who wrote the letter or where it was sent to. He actually thought he'd solve it and find that Sandra girl and she'd get her treasure...or he would take it if she wasn't around anymore.

There were times that letter caused a lot of arguments between us. I told him if he didn't stop fretting over it day and night I was going to rip it to pieces. One day he simply gave up and said he was done with it. I forgot all about it until you just brought it up now."

"Well, it is sort of interesting," Donald acknowledged. "Anyway, I'll take this stuff home and look at it when I have more time. I'm out of here unless you need anything else."

"No, just be careful. I'll call you as soon as I know

exactly when my sister is ready for me so you can take me and my little collection of bags and boxes on over to her place, okay?"

"Okay, Ma. I'll probably be back before then and I'll call some places to see who wants the furniture and other stuff. Love you, Ma," Donald said as he leaned over and gave her a kiss on her forehead. He put on his jacket and walked over to the front door.

"You too," she said hastily as the theme music for *Edge of Night* came on and instantly drew her back into her story world.

CHAPTER 16

After locking the front door of his mother's house, Donald D'Angelo walked the two blocks back to his car. He no sooner pulled out of the parking space than a replacement vehicle was backing in and claiming its new-found rights to the precious territory. Donald headed toward the Schuylkill Expressway, then up the winding Wissahickon to his stately old stone home just off Lincoln Drive. He had bought the home eight years ago when he was still married and had very young children. The home was all that was left now. The wife and the children were gone. They lived in New Jersey, far enough away from his on-again/off-again drinking problem, but still close enough for the children to visit when it was under control.

The house was in a good location for him. It was a convenient ride to his parents' house in South Philly, and only about twenty minutes to the bookstore he managed in Chestnut Hill. Now that his mother was moving out to

Delaware County he began thinking about whether or not it made sense to continue living there. The house was too big for just one person and it cost a fortune to heat in the winter. He had thought about giving it up many times, but he loved old stone homes in old neighborhoods with old curbside trees that canopied the roadways below. It was so different from the jammed-up rows of narrow homes where he grew up in South Philly. He would give it some more thought later.

When he got home he gathered up the mail that sat in a small pile just under the slot in the front door. He sorted through it quickly then stuffed all of it under his armpit as he grabbed a soda out of the fridge and a handful of pretzels. He adjusted the thermostat to warm up the house a little since he kept it low all day in an effort to save money. Then, he went upstairs to the bedroom, took off his clothes, put on a pair of flannel pajama bottoms and a t-shirt.

TV on, covers pulled down; the mail, the soda and the pretzels all on the nightstand...he was dug in for the evening. Sometime before midnight, usually, he'd be asleep for the next several hours in whatever position he was in just before consciousness left him. It was a normal night for Donald, home alone as always.

It was around 2 o'clock when he woke up. He had to pee. But something else had stirred him, too. He stood in front of the toilet and as he relieved himself he began thinking about the letter in his father's Navy box. That was all it took, just a minute of pondering about the letter to Sandra and he was wide awake. It was as if the letter was calling to him and his curiosity was too strong to resist.

He put on slippers and went downstairs, out the side door to the driveway and opened the trunk of the car. There, he rummaged through his father's box and pulled out the notebook with the letter inside.

It was cold outside and he was in just his pajamas. He slammed the trunk shut and hurried inside and back upstairs where he buried most of himself under the covers, shivering for another minute or so. The TV was still on. He turned it off.

Donald fluffed up the two pillows he had on the bed and stacked them behind him so he could sit up straight. He then opened the notebook and took out the letter. Now, in the bright light of his bedroom, he saw how fragile it was.

Half the envelope had been burned away and the letter itself was written on paper that was now dry and brittle. The paper had begun tearing along its folded seams. Right away, Donald thought he would buy a plastic sleeve in the morning and keep the letter inside it. For now, he simply laid it atop a magazine so it would lie flat.

He noticed the handwriting was very neat and easy to read. At the very bottom of the letter was a stamped marking that said "approved" and there were some scribbled initials just under it. This, of course, was where a commanding officer indicated he had reviewed the letter for any sensitive material, and then cleared it for delivery. But Donald, unfamiliar with that particular military procedure, had no idea that's what it meant. He studied the initials briefly but they were illegible. He decided to ignore it all and began to read the letter.

November 18, 1943

Dear Sandra,
So much has changed since my last day at home. I
hardly think I am the same person. In fact, I <u>know</u> I
am not the same person. I have so many fond
memories of our little rural town—our farm, my
parents and friends, Eddie and Uncle Tim and, of
course, you. I saw you standing in the window of
your father's store when we were pulling out. Oh
that I could erase what has happened and bring all
the good times back, I would. But now I have
traveled clear across the country from the Atlantic to
the Pacific and my ticket is not marked for a return
trip. At this moment we are at sea and there is the
cold reality that many of us, including me, may not
be here on this good earth much longer. I have
accepted my mortality and actually think it may be
the only way to end the misery I suffer. How I wish
that it were different. How I wish that it has not
become so difficult for me to want to survive and
return to you. But what I learned the day I left you
prevents my coming back. My only recourse to all
my horror is revenge. It is my temperament, you
know that. It will be the only thing that lives on
after I die. You must accept it and know that I
loved you more than anything in the world, ever,
and that losing you was the one thing I would not
accept. And so, my dearest Sandra, since it is
unlikely we shall ever be together again, I have left

you a treasure—a treasure you valued more than me. It is a priceless token of my devotion to you and what length I would go to, to mourn the end of our love. War is just not here before me in this strange part of the world. It was there, too, on the banks of the river I loved, disguised so I would never see it coming. Just as the enemy here is disguised, but I know it is coming. And, as it did at home, the enemy here will destroy me, too. Go now and look for your treasure. It will make everything clear. It will put an ending on the story. It will free you from not understanding why I have changed. Rev up Uncle Tim's old motor like I taught you and travel the roads we took to our castle. But leave the net behind and take a shovel instead. You'll not be capturing jimmies this day. Find the tree along the back side, the one we cut to remember our magical day. On the opposite side, just a foot or two away, begin your dig and take, my love, what I have left for you. It will be difficult, given what I know now, to force myself to forget it all and make our last day together, when we ran wild in the rain, the final memory I will be holding onto when the last breath escapes my body and sets me free from all that has happened.

R

"What the hell?" was the first thought that came to Donald as he finished reading the letter. He went back and read it again, this time more slowly. The letter was not only mysterious, it was downright bizarre! Realizing that his father was probably the only person, other than the letter's author, who had ever seen its contents, made him understand why his father was so obsessed with it. No one, Donald thought to himself, could read this letter and not wonder about it.

Was it a love letter? Was it a hate letter? Was it a suicide letter? Donald couldn't make up his mind what the hell it was. All he knew was that he had an incredibly compulsive feeling come over him that he was meant to pick up where his father left off. He would find out who Sandra was. He would find out who "R" was. And, he would find out not only where, but what, the treasure was.

CHAPTER 17

The alarm clock went off at exactly seven o'clock in the morning. It pulsed a rhythmic tone, relentless in its mission to arouse whatever slept within its audible range. At first, the repetitive beat worked its way into Donald's dream. It was a drummer beating his drum in a passing parade, then it seamlessly transitioned into a hammer that a carpenter was using to build a bookcase at Donald's store. He asked the carpenter to stop but the man ignored him. The hammering went on and on until, gradually, Donald's immerging consciousness began making sense of it all. As he came to, he reached over and hit the snooze button on top of his clock, relieved when the annoying hammering had stopped. He immediately fell back to sleep, but only for ten minutes when the entire process recycled itself and began pounding the room once more. This time, however, Donald rose immediately. He slammed the off button on the alarm and swung his feet out from under the covers and onto the floor. Another day was about to begin. But not just another day. No, this day would be different. This day would signal the start of a journey.

Donald had fallen asleep with his father's Navy box still on the bed. The letter to the mystery woman, Sandra, along with his father's notebook, lay on top of the undisturbed second pillow next to him. Donald glanced over at the letter. The second he saw it, he immediately felt consumed by its presence. He picked it up and began reading it once more. He found no relief from its puzzlement when he finished. He put the letter down and began his morning routine. But this morning he did not turn on the television. He did not want to be distracted. He automatically went through his usual drill of shaving, brushing his teeth, showering and getting dressed with no thought to any of these tasks. His entire mind was focused on the letter.

Little town, father's store, river, farm, castle. All these items from the letter kept cluttering Donald's thoughts as he attempted to decipher their meaning and the writer's intent.

Even while he was in his car driving to work, he found himself preoccupied with the letter. The radio was turned off, getting its first rest since Donald bought the car a few months ago. Usually, if the engine was on, so too was the radio. And so the day went. Donald went through all the usual motions at work. He took care of customer needs, restocked some shelves, and did a little bookkeeping. Never once did he stop thinking about the letter. He could not wait to get home and devote his entire attention to it.

Coming home to an empty house was the worst punishment his drinking had forced him to endure. Donald missed having a family, especially during sober times when everything was practically picture perfect. But that was gone now. He could wish it back all he wanted, but he knew that part of his life was over. The future? Well, just as it did in the past, his drinking problem, and how he chose to deal with it, would direct his future. He had been sober for 26 months, long enough to feel some progress, but short enough to know he was still vulnerable.

He pulled into his driveway, parked the car and grabbed the bag of fast food he had picked up on the way home. Inside, he changed into his nighttime uniform of flannel pajama pants and a t-shirt. He then grabbed the letter and the notebook off the bed and took them downstairs to the kitchen table.

Donald had bought a packet of clear plastic sleeves at the office store earlier that day. He took one out, separated the pocket and inserted the letter inside. He felt better now that the letter at least had a little protection. Now he could unwrap his dinner while he read the letter once more.

By now he had it just about memorized. He was, however, absolutely no further along in interpreting what it said. He put it down and picked up his father's notebook.

When he first glanced at the notebook at his mother's house, he thought it merely contained several pages of lists his father had made, based on information in the letter. There were lists for state names or whose abbreviations ended in the letter "D." Then there was a list of river names for each state. There were lists of postal zones and various lists of other postal information. That's about all that Donald had originally thought was in the notebook so he hadn't paid much attention to it. But now, he realized there was more.

In the back half of the book, his father had kept a diary of his thoughts about the letter and the results of his search for its intended recipient or the identity of its sender. This information, Donald thought, might be a tremendous help in getting him caught up to where his father was at the time he abandoned the mission.

The first thing his father did was to list all the possible individual clues in the letter. These were written on several pages, leaving room under each for comments his father made. The list and comments appeared as follows:

Clues in the Letter:
- people mentioned: Sandra, Uncle Tim, Eddie and R
- Sandra's father had a store
- R is a Marine
- R was on a ship when he wrote the letter...It's dated November 17, 1943.

Because I personally picked up the bag that contained the letter, I know that it was off-loaded from the troop transport Doyen. The Doyen had come under fire when it was landing troops onto Tarawa. There was damage to the ship's mail room and since the letter's envelope was scorched, I assume it got that way because of the attack on the ship. There is also the possibility that the letter originated on some other ship and it wound up onboard the Doyen because it eventually would be going back to the U.S. It had been in port in New Zealand and that is where it could have picked up mail from other ships in the fleet. I am making a fairly calculated guess, from what I have learned about the attack on Tarawa, and knowing that the Doyen was there and that R's letter was on the ship...I think R was among the Marines who landed at Tarawa. I have no idea whether or not he survived the battle. Bodies of many Marines who were killed were never recovered so there is no real confirmation sometimes. R says he travelled from Atlantic to Pacific. ...meaning he came from the east coast I guess.

The Treasure:
- priceless, token of his devotion
- something Sandra values more than him

Is he serious or is joking? Sounds like maybe it is a piece of jewelry of some sort. Maybe it was an engagement ring he had intended to give her when he got back. And if he didn't survive the war, well this was a way he could still see that she got it. A ring would be a token of his devotion and his asking her to marry him might be what she valued more than anything. Or it could mean something entirely different since it is not clear if the object is something she valued more than him, himself... or if it was something that she valued more than he valued it. This is confusing.

- there is a river in his home town ...At least I know to look for a town or city that has a river nearby
- rev up Uncle Tim's motor the way I taught you
This is was probably a car or a truck? Motorcycle? Who knows, but it must have been hard to start and he taught her the trick to get it going.
- roads to hidden castle.
I guess the location is at or near some kind of castle. I don't know of any castles in this country except that hamburger joint over in Jersey...maybe they hung out at a hamburger stand...or maybe it's a building that looks like a castle, or some other store that has "castle" as part of its name.
- don't need a net...not be capturing Jimmies
What are jimmies? The only jimmies I know are those chocolate sprinkles you put on ice cream or cake. It doesn't make sense. If you catch them with a net, maybe it is a word for some kind of animal. Maybe they chased butterflies at the castle and they called them jimmies. I don't think this clue is going to help much.
- bring a shovel ...based on this, I guess the treasure is buried.
-Tree they cut   ...He says the tree is on the backside of the building, close by and they cut it down. So maybe

the stump is still there depending on what he means by
"cut."
- dig a foot or two away on opposite side
- last day together ran wild in the rain

Clues on the Envelope:
- 'C' appears to be the first letter of the name of the city
- 'D' appears to be the last letter of the name of the state
or the abbreviation of a state.
This means it could be any of the following:
Maryland, Rhode Island, or Idaho.
- the word 'Free' is written where the stamp usually
goes in the upper corner...this means it was military
mail and a stamp wasn't necessary.

Donald put the letter next to the list of clues in his
father's notebook, checking to see if his father had missed
any. He hadn't. Donald could tell his father was as curious
as he was about the letter and it was obvious he had put a
lot of thought into solving its puzzle. Donald decided the
first logical thing to do was determine what state the letter
was originally addressed to. There seemed to be enough
information in the letter to narrow the list.

Making the assumption that R's hometown was on the
east coast, that would eliminate Idaho and North and South
Dakota, states whose abbreviations ended in "d." That left
Maryland and Rhode Island. Donald thought this was a
pretty good discovery until he found that his father had
already narrowed down the search to those two states. Plus,

Donald noticed on his father's list of state abbreviations, North and South Dakota were not abbreviated by their initials back in the 1940s. He knew his father was very intelligent and his failure to acknowledge that made him feel stupid. He realized the best thing he could do, would be to simply take the time to read the entire notebook. Otherwise, he would be wasting time thinking about questions his father more than likely had already resolved.

Donald cleaned up the kitchen table and emptied the sink of dirty dishes. He made a cup of decaf, threw a few cookies on a plate, picked up the notebook and the letter and proceeded upstairs to the bedroom. There, he would fluff up the pillows on the bed and camp out for the rest of the night, reading his father's notebook until he fell asleep.

CHAPTER 18

Fifty-six-year-old Louise Henderson Wheeler sat in the old rocker on the front porch of the family home. She had just watched the final episode of a sitcom on television called Laverne & Shirley. Now, she would sit for awhile and enjoy the fresh spring evening until she was ready for bed. Then she would return inside the house, change into a nightgown and fall asleep watching the late news.

It was a big house. Her father helped her grandfather build it. There was an addition built on later as the family grew. Louise lived there alone now. It was not too many years before that the house was overrun with family. Her mother and father ruled the roost. Louise and her husband, Hank, lived there for the first four years of their marriage. Then the two of them purchased a house just down the street. Louise' sister, Sandra, always had lived in the house. All of the family, except Hank, at one time or another worked at the family hardware store. Louise had little interest in the store and didn't enjoy working there, but it was expected of her so she, too, made her contribution to the family enterprise.

Hank was a devout waterman on the Chesapeake; he reeked of oysters and crabs most days and had the rough and scarred hands like so many others of his trade. In the off season, he worked at the poultry packinghouse a few miles outside of town on Church Hill Road. Then, the aroma of fresh-killed chicken permeated his work clothes. Accordingly, Louise always had to separate Hank's laundry from any other in the household.

Oddly, there were no children living in the house now. The last child to tear up and down the stairs, slam doors and avoid any household chores was Sandra's son, RJ. He had grown up and left. He had his own family now and lived in the big city on the other side of the Bay.

Louise's parents and Sandra were all gone now. So, too, was Hank. He was always sort of a drifter and then one day he just drifted away forever. Louise didn't mind. After a few years of marriage, Hank was never around much and there had never been any children he was responsible for. He did show up one time later to process divorce papers. That was the last they saw of each other.

So, here sat Louise, alone and lonely, on the front porch of what was now her house. She had sold the hardware store to a large chain. As a symbol of the love she had for her sister, Louise took a major portion of the money she made from the sale and invested it in RJ. She arranged for her father's old accountant, known to everyone in the family as *Uncle* Bert, to set RJ up in his own development company. What funds from the sale of the store were left after that would be more than enough to support Louise's simple lifestyle for the rest of her life. Sandra was a great loss to Louise. They were born just two years apart and had grown up together. They had become very close. There wasn't a story untold or a secret not kept between them. They knew absolutely everything about each other...well, maybe almost everything.

Louise had no interest in pursuing someone new to share her life with. Oh, there were plenty of men who would accidentally-on-purpose wind up "just being in the neighborhood" but she couldn't care less. Most of them, she felt, were probably more interested in her new-found wealth. So, here she sat, building her reputation as the town's rich old spinster who spent much of her time in the old rocker on the front porch of her house, showing no interest in anything or anybody.

The Harris Farm, meanwhile, had seen better days. There were no interested offspring to pass it on to, so Robert's father sold it off in parcels to neighboring farmers and what little was left sat decaying and uncared for. Robert's father was in a nursing home across the Bay near Annapolis. He wasn't able to take care of himself anymore. He seemed, however, to enjoy listening to music and watching TV with some of the other men in the home. His wife, meanwhile, was in the next building over, across the lawn from his room's window. She didn't remember who he was anymore. Most days she sat in a wheelchair parked on the sun porch. There, she would stare out the window and ask anyone who happened to pass by if they had seen

Robert...but if you asked her who Robert was, she didn't know.

*****

RJ and some of his company's colleagues walked a few blocks from their downtown office to Baltimore's inner harbor. There, RJ's 35-foot Chris-Craft cabin cruiser sat motionless inside a slip. The men boarded the boat and RJ took the helm as they motored out through the harbor into the Patapsco River and then into the Chesapeake Bay. The boat's name could be easily read by those sitting in the dockside restaurant watching as it pulled away. In bright red script across the width of the transom were the words, *Hardware Lady*.

Once out into the Chesapeake, the boat cut almost directly across the bay to the Eastern Shore and then made its way up the Chester River an into the Corsica. It was a beautiful day on the bay. RJ and his colleagues were in no hurry. It would take an hour or so to reach their destination about two-thirds of the way up the Corsica River.

"Now, I ask you, isn't this better than driving over like we usually do?" RJ commented as he leaned back and looked at his guests sitting on the bright blue cushions that lined the aft seating area.

RJ was owner and president of The Corsica Development Company. With him were his chief architect, a marine engineer consultant and a local surveyor who intimately knew the "math" of the area. RJ's company had purchased several tracts of waterfront property just off the

Corsica, up a small tributary known as the Alder Branch. Here, he would eventually fulfill his primary ambition since his mother's death. Here, he would build a beautifully crafted residential community and marina, a tribute to his mother and father.

This would be RJ's final review of the property from the water. By now, he had walked the grounds many times as the company's plans for the new development were being laid out. All the zoning and pre-development issues had been taken care of and the clearing of the landsite was about to begin. An important feature of the residential property would be its marina where residents would have a complete luxury facility and dockage for their boats.

As the cruiser steered just inside the entrance of the Alder Branch, RJ slowed the motor and turned up the volume on his depth finder. The space between the beeps it sounded grew increasingly shorter as the bottom of the river rose. These were shallow waters and running aground was a definite threat, especially at this time of day when high tide was still hours off. They stayed in the middle of the waterway, slowly trolling farther up the branch. Meanwhile, the surveyor was holding open a large chart on the table in the center of the salon. He'd look at the chart, then along the shoreline until he had found the spot he was looking for. He asked RJ to stop the boat and hold the position. There wasn't a need to drop anchor; the current was barely moving.

"This is your shorefront, Mr. Henderson," the surveyor told RJ. "It runs from that large outgrowth of trees there, all the way up to where that little sandbar juts out."

RJ scanned the view, one that he had seen many times by now. He turned to the engineer.

"So, what do you think, Frank? Can we dredge the entire line and build a channel out to the center here?

"I don't see why not. It shouldn't be too difficult; it's a soft bottom. The residents may have to dredge again, but that'll be another decade or more years down the road. What do you plan to do about that old dock and boatshed that's tucked in that marsh area?"

The sun was getting intense by now and there were few clouds in the sky. RJ put his hand up to his forehead to shade his eyes as he looked across the water at the boatshed.

"John and I debated that a few weeks ago," RJ said of his chief architect. "I thought maybe it would add a little quaint touch to the marina if we let it stand and rehabbed it. John didn't think it was worth the trouble so he convinced me otherwise."

"Yeah it just wasn't going to marry well with the fuel dock that has to go right there," John added. "Plus, it'd be too fragile if we tried moving it; she'd probably crumble the minute we touched it anyway. So kiss it goodbye."

John took out his camera and began taking a series of pictures along the property line from one end to the other. The design for the marina was pretty much complete, but there were some cosmetic elements he wanted to add now that he could see the site from the water. He turned to the engineering consultant.

"How soon do you think we can begin dredging and cleaning out the shoreline?"

"Oh, probably within a few weeks. Depends on how

fast we can pull permits and get a dredger in," the engineer responded. "You can go ahead and plan on tearing out everything on the frontage—the trees, the boatshed and what's left of the old pilings. That won't be much to do. Then you can start the new footings."

"The marina will really make the place," RJ commented. "It's important that we complete it even before all the models are open. It will practically pre-sell the homesites as soon as the boaters see it." He then turned and took his position at the helm and began turning the boat around.

"I know a good place for lunch. Let's head over there," RJ suggested. Then he looked at the surveyor.

"When do you think that old boatshed was built?" he asked.

"I'm just guessing, but based on its construction and what's left of it, I'd say it was put up sometime around the 1920s-30s. The property there used to be a farm but I doubt that the waterfront area was ever used. It has probably just sat there like that for years. Most farmers didn't have big boats. The owner might have had the shed built so he could rent it out and make a little extra money; that'd be my guess."

By now RJ's cruiser had reached the Corsica River. To port, a few minutes east, was the small town of Centreville. RJ put the boat to starboard and headed back toward the Chesapeake Bay and Baltimore on the other side.

RJ was anxious to get his new project underway. He anticipated that "Alder Cove and Marina" would be sold out once construction was completed on the first section.

CHAPTER 19

After several weeks embedded into an entirely new lifestyle, Donald D'Angelo felt like a new man. It was all because of the dead letter he had found in his father's old Navy box. His life was no longer a day-to-day slog through a job he had lost interest in, a drinking problem that constantly challenged him and a loss of his loved ones that only depressed him. No, now that the letter had come into his life, everything had changed. It gave him something to look forward to during every minute of his free time. He was absorbed by its contents as if each little element was a part or fixture of some new hobby he had taken up and become totally enamored of. He would tinker endlessly with every minute detail, looking at it from all sides and researching its meaning and relationship to all the other parts and to the whole.

Working at the bookstore had provided him access to

numerous resources he could use, from an atlas to numerous history and social publications. He disregarded some of the stocking guidelines at the store so he could order books that he thought might help in his research. As frustrated as he was that he had not developed any new discoveries beyond those already made by his father, he had no hesitation to keep digging and pursuing answers for all the clues. He was simply happy to have the challenge in his life that the letter presented. In fact, he was far enough along in the project that he was a little worried about what would happen when the puzzle was solved and the treasure found. What would he do then? It wasn't like he could simply go to the post office and ask for another dead letter, especially another one with a treasure hunt.

As his father had, Donald concentrated on Rhode Island and Maryland. One of them, they were sure, was where Sandra lived. His father seemed to imply that he favored Rhode Island, but Donald wasn't sure why. It was just a feeling he got from reading his father's notes.

What his mother hadn't told him was how contentious his father's obsession with the letter had become. He learned this only by random comments his father made in the notebook. Just as it had with Donald, the letter was consuming all of his father's spare time. His mother was not happy. For a few weeks or even months maybe it was okay. But after a year of her husband's intense concentration on little else she had finally had it. Repairs around the house were left undone. Among them, the roof had a serious leak and the toilet took forever to refill. The car needed work and was barely running. Meanwhile, his father seldom finished a meal. He gobbled up enough to hold him and then took off back to his desk and his sacred letter.

When his father finally announced he was going to take some vacation time and go to Rhode Island to investigate the clues in the letter, his mother put her foot down. She told him if he spent good vacation time and even a dime of what little money they had on some wild goose chase to Rhode Island, he shouldn't expect to find her at home when he got back. She meant it. He knew it.

It was at this time that Donald's father seemed to run out of steam. He stopped making diary entries in his notebook. Nothing seemed to have been done thereafter. He apparently put the letter and the notebook into the Navy box and that was the end of it until after he died and Donald took up the cause.

But Donald could do what his father could not. There was no one to stop him from going to Rhode Island if he wanted to.

While he was on his lunch break, Donald decided he'd act on an idea he had for awhile. He walked several stores down from the bookstore to the travel agency. He knew the agent; he had used her when he booked the few times he traveled, and she was a regular customer in the bookstore.

"Hey Dorothy, how you doing?" he said as he walked inside, the electronic door chime ding-dong-dinging as he entered.

"Just fine, Donald. What brings you in? Are you planning a trip somewhere?" Dorothy asked back.

"I'm not sure. I've developed an interest in castles and

maybe you can help me. Do you know of any actual castles that may be in Rhode Island or Maryland?"

"Wow, that's this week's weird customer request. But oddly enough I know there are some castles in Rhode Island. I don't know about any in Maryland."

"Really?" Donald asked somewhat startled. "Tell me more"

"I'll tell you what, I'm in the middle of arranging some flights for someone and I'd have to make a phone call or two to find out about the castles. Why don't you stop by on your way home later today and I'll see what I can put together for you."

"That would be fine. Oh, one other thing since I am already the weird customer for the week. I'm primarily interested in castles that are in rural areas, not large cities or heavily populated areas, and there must be a river nearby. I'll stop by around 5:30. Is that a good time?" Donald asked.

"I'll put my best person on the job—me! See you later," said Dorothy.

At first, Donald hadn't paid much attention to the castle clue. He thought it was a little too obscure. But the more he thought about it, the more he became convinced that its obscurity was perhaps a plus. There must not be too many castles around, he thought, which meant that might quickly narrow the search, especially if he could find a castle near a small, rural town that had a river nearby. "Nothin' to it," he jokingly thought to himself. But, as Donald had already discovered, sometimes what appeared simple proved to be quite difficult. He'd wait to see what

Dorothy came up with.

The rest of the afternoon went slowly. It was a rainy day in Chestnut Hill and that kept the after-school rush down to a crawl. On nice days, parents picking up their kids would often stop in the book store to kill a little time and keep them occupied. Donald didn't mind helping with the babysitting since the hour or so usually included several purchases. He would often grab the latest children's book, sit squat on the floor and read to the kids while they sat circled around him. It was something he dearly missed from the past when he used to read to his own children at bedtime every night.

When it rained, the parents didn't want the parking hassle and then having to hustle the kids back and forth between downpours. On days like this, they went directly home instead.

So, Donald grabbed a copy of the latest James Michener best seller, *Space,* off the front table, plopped himself down in one of the big stuffed chairs in the center of the store and spent most of the afternoon reading. When the part-time evening clerk came in he left for the night and headed down the street to the travel agency.

"So Dorothy, did you find any castles for me?" Donald asked as he walked in.

"You'd be surprised, although I didn't locate any with a moat and live crocodiles," she joked as she handed a list to Donald.

"There are more in Maryland than I ever would imagine, but most of them are pretty close to Baltimore so they don't fit the criteria you gave me. But you may want to check some of them out. I'm having some brochures mailed to me. I should have them in a couple of days for you. Now, Rhode Island is a different story, maybe because it's a small state and there aren't a lot of big cities there."

"Well, good," Donald responded. "What kind of castles did you find in Rhode Island?"

Dorothy pointed to the list she had handed Donald.

"Actually it might make a nice little vacation because most of them are close by each other. They're clustered in the Newport area on Narragansett Bay. Lots of water and boats, though I'd go in the fall when the leaves are turning. That would probably be spectacular."

"If I go, I suspect it will be soon, so I'll have to forfeit all the color," Donald said.

"There is one castle a little north, more rural, in a little village called Wickford in what's called North Kingstown. It's on a cove that leads out to the main harbor and I'm told there's a creek that is large enough that it could be called a river. I'm having materials on it and the castles in Newport sent so you can take a look. Many of these places don't really look like castles, but they are quite large and extravagant. Some were summer homes for the very rich."

"This is working out fine. I need a few days to figure out what I want to do. By the time all those brochures come I should be close to planning a few days up there. Give me a call at the store and let me know when everything is in and I'll come get it," Donald told her.

"Oh, don't worry. I'll probably bring them with me on my next visit to the bookstore. I should be ready for a new read by then."

Donald was anxious to get home. He had names of castles and basic locations. He could plot them on his maps and see if any were worth a visit. He was excited.

When he arrived home he followed his usual routine. He crashed some dinner together, this time a can of soup and a sandwich he made from cold cuts he had in the fridge. When he was done, he cleared off the table and spread open the map he had of the State of Maryland. Then he took Dorothy's list and began looking for the castle locations and marking them on the map. This was proving to be a frustrating endeavor. The castles, whether they were real or not, all seemed to be located in populated areas. Many were close to Baltimore just as Dorothy had warned. Others were in small towns, but there were no rivers to be seen nearby. Given his father's and his "gut feelings" that somehow Rhode Island was the state they should pay attention to, he folded the Maryland map and then spread open the one for Rhode Island.

There were a good 8-to-10 so-called castles in and around Newport. He would have to wait for the brochures to come to really see what they were. He figured some of them just might be commercial operations, like hotels or restaurants that had a castle name and were not actually a real castle. He also noticed the one in North Kingstown that Dorothy had mentioned. He marked each castle on the map and then he drew a circle around each, roughly 50 miles in diameter. He thought since R and Sandra lived near the castle it probably wouldn't be much farther than 25 miles away. Then he searched for a small town with a name that began with a "C."

He spotted Charlestown off to the southwest, but there was no river nearby. Cranston was to the north, but was pretty much part of the busy Providence area. And again, he saw no river near Cranston. He kept looking. Off to the northwest of Newport and even closer to North Kingstown was a small town named Coventry. Close by, traveling from west to east, there was a small meandering body of water. On Donald's map it had no name, but it sure looked like a river.

CHAPTER 20

It wasn't long before Donald had a stack of brochures about the various castles in Rhode Island. Some of them turned out to be hotels or small inns tucked back in rural settings overlooking Rhode Island Sound or Narragansett Bay. These were castles in name only.

Others were expansive homesteads whose main residence was called a castle, or at least popularly referred to as such. These did not take on the appearance of typical European medieval structures with round turrets, moats and defensive portals. Instead, these castles had become famous historical landmarks, often built by very wealthy American industrialists near the turn of the twentieth century. Any of them could well have been the castle to which R referred to in his letter. They all had elaborately landscaped grounds which no doubt harbored a number of secluded romantic settings where R and Sandra could hide from the world.

Luckily, the castles in Rhode Island that Donald put on his list to visit were in close proximity to each other and all within a reasonable driving distance from the town of Coventry. Plus, there were lots of waterways everywhere.

Coventry itself appeared a good prospect as the hometown of R and Sandra. There were two bodies of water close by. One was the Flat River Reservoir. It fed the Pawtuxet River, which meandered northeasterly until it eventually dumped into the Providence River just north of Narragansett Bay.

So, Donald had uncovered a small town whose name began with a "C" in a state that ended in "D" and there was a river nearby along with several castles less than an hour's drive away. In addition to these favorable items, he had read that farms were very much a part of the Rhode Island landscape in the 1940s, especially farms famous for raising Rhode Island Reds. These were chickens selectively bred to serve two profitable markets: one being a good consumer appetite for a rich-flavored stewing bird and the other for brown eggs.

Donald set aside a few vacation days plus one of his off weekends and was planning to use this time for the trip to Rhode Island. He decided it would be cheaper to drive and, besides, he would need a car once he got there anyway. Philadelphia to Rhode Island is about a five-and-a-half hour drive. Donald planned to use Saturday as a travel day and then the next three for exploring the castles and the town of Coventry. On the final day he'd return home. Of course, he thought, if he found the treasure and if it was something very valuable, that could change everything.

On the Saturday morning of what Donald now referred to as his *treasure hunt*, he went to the supermarket, then the drug store and picked up a few things for his trip. Next, he stopped at the hardware store and bought a shovel and a pair of work gloves. When he got back home, he packed a bag of clothes and other essentials and tossed it into the trunk of his Ford Tempo. The shovel was too long for the trunk. He threw that in the back seat. Next, he filled a lunch bag with things to snack on during the drive and made a thermos of coffee. Then, he walked through the house making sure all the windows and doors were locked and the faucets turned off tight. He left a couple of lights on, including the porch light, locked the side door to the driveway, got in his car and headed for Interstate 95 North. Next to him, on the passenger's seat, were his father's notebook, a new one he had started for himself and a stack of brochures and some road maps bound by a rubber band. Now, after months of research and rereading the dead letter and his father's notes an endless amount of times, Donald was excited and ready for high adventure...or at least considerably more adventure than he had experienced in years.

Donald arrived in Rhode Island late in the afternoon. He had planned to look for a place to stay near the intersection of I-95 and State Route 4. This was a good central location, putting him between Coventry and Newport where most of the castles were. Around 5:30 he exited 95 and pulled into a small roadside inn where he got a room. After he unloaded the car, he walked over to the inn's restaurant and had dinner. He decided he would spend the rest of the night reviewing the brochures and then going to bed early. He had been driving most of the day and he was tired, but still very much energized to get on with the treasure hunt first thing in the morning.

There were four castles that Donald had decided to investigate. Three were located in the Newport area; the fourth was the one in nearby North Kingstown. His plan was to visit each location and attempt to tour the grounds on the back side. Here he would look for an old tree stump or signs of anything that could be interpreted as a "cut tree" as described in R's letter.

Donald ate a quick breakfast at the inn and then got in his car and drove south on Route 4, then over Route 138 to Newport. The first stop was Belcourt Castle. According to the brochure, it was built in the early 1890's by Oliver Hazard Perry Belmont, a bachelor at the time who apparently had more interest in horses than finding a wife. He did, however, eventually marry one of the renowned Vanderbilts, or at least the former wife of one. Her first husband was William Kissam Vanderbilt who, oddly enough, was Oliver Belmont's friend and business partner.

The entire ground floor of Belcourt Castle housed stables for Belmont's prize coach horses in addition to facilities for his elaborate collection of carriages. Of note is that the Belmont Stakes, one of the three horse races representing the sport's Triple Crown is named after Oliver Belmont. The castle had subsequent owners and it had fallen into decay for many years before it was later restored. During World War II, at the time R and Sandra may have visited, the ground floor was being rented to the Federal government and served as a repair facility for military equipment.

Donald had second thoughts about not going inside Belcourt Castle. Its architecture and museum furnishing were something he would certainly have an interest in seeing, but time was of the essence. He needed to spend as much time as possible walking the grounds looking for whatever would fit R's clue about a cut tree. He did not pass up the opportunity of questioning any representative of the Castle that he came across. He found nothing, however. If he was questioned why he was randomly roaming the grounds looking for a tree stump, he simply answered that it was a meeting place during his parents' courtship and he just wanted to see if what they had so often talked about was still in existence.

Donald left Belcourt and drove to The Breakers, just a few minutes north. The Breakers was not formally named as a castle, though such a reference to its grandeur was not out of the question. R and Sandra may have easily called it a castle given its scale and elaborate grounds, not to mention a majestic view of Easton Bay.

The Breakers was the summer home of Cornelius Vanderbilt II, built in 1893-95. Like all the great mansions of its era, the Breakers is testimony to American extravagance and industry at the turn of the century. The interior, which features 70 rooms, is a showcase of Italian and African marble and rich woods from around the world. The Breakers Stable and Carriage House, a half-mile west of the main mansion, were state-of-the art in their time. The gardens surrounding the main property feature an elaborate collection of foreign and domestic trees with strategically planted shrubs and flower beds accenting their magnificence.

It took Donald twice as much time to tour the grounds of The Breakers, but he was left with the same result as Belcourt.

Castle Hill was Donald's next stop. This was a summer "lab" built in 1875 by a famous Harvard scientist by the name of Alexander Agassiz whose fame and riches came mostly from the mining industry. He took a badly failing Michigan copper mine and turned it into the world's most prosperous. Quite the innovator for his time, Agassiz installed safety devices at the mine, and even provided pensions and accident funds for his miners. But mining wasn't his only interest. Agassiz was a marine biologist of some acclaim and had set up an elaborate laboratory at his Rhode Island home. The Castle Hill Lighthouse stands embedded in the cliff rock nearby, overlooking a spectacular view of where Narragansett Bay meets the Atlantic. The main building was leased to Navy officers and their wives during World War II, when and if R and Sandra may have been in the neighborhood. After the war, Castle Hill was transformed into a guest inn.

Donald's luck did not change at Castle Hill. After an hour of walking the grounds, he left and set out for his final tour, Smith's Castle. This was a longer drive, first back west on Route 138 and then up on U.S. 1 a few miles to North Kingstown.

Looking like anything but a castle, Smith's Castle was the oldest on Donald's list. It was built in 1678 and is also one of the oldest private homes in Rhode Island. Its builder, Roger Smith, had fortifications built into the home's structure which is how it earned its nickname as a castle. Smith's Castle had nothing like the grandeur of the other homes Donald had visited. It was basically a rectangular, two-story clapboard structure with a large chimney emerging from the center of the roof. One thing Smith's Castle did have was a dense wooded area behind the house. It would take Donald the rest of the afternoon to scour the grounds.

By now, he had discovered what he had already pretty much realized during his search back at Belcourt Castle that morning. And, this was the fact that he was attempting to locate a very small landmark that stood forty years ago. Any number of things could have altered its appearance by now, even if, indeed, it still existed at all. He had hoped to find an exposed tree stump, one that had stood through the years. He saw one at Smith's Castle, but it barely poked above ground level and was covered by dirt and grass. So it was difficult to determine how old it was. There were other spots, too, that looked suspicious. They may have at one time been occupied by a mighty oak or spruce, but it was hard to tell. By four o'clock he decided to call it a day. He had left himself plenty of time to pursue other clues tomorrow in Coventry.

CHAPTER 21

The bright green Jeep Wagoneer pulled off the gravel roadway as the driver shifted into four-wheel drive. It then began weaving its own pathway in and around aged trees of all sizes and between walls of thick overgrowth left untouched for decades. The driver tossed and turned the vehicle farther into the wooded area until he was forced to stop. Ahead, about 100 yards, the waters of the Alder Branch of the Corsica River peeked through the openings in the trees. Two men emerged from the vehicle, walked around to the back and dropped open the rear gate. Then, they began unloading their gear, which included sets of chaining pins, range poles, a level and a transit, a tripod and various other pieces of equipment.

The two men would begin several days of surveying the property and determining fence lines. Rolls of chain link fence and steel poles were already strapped to flatbed trucks now making their way here to a new construction site. A bulldozer, backhoe and a parade of dump trucks were standing by just a few miles away. These were awaiting the order to come clear the land and prepare it for the initial stage of homes that would rise almost overnight and become a community called Alder Cove and Marina. Much of the land here had more than likely remained untouched since the tribes of the Algonquin Indians had raised food in its soil and fished from its river banks.

"Every time I do a location like this I sort of feel a little guilty," the one surveyor said to the other. "It's so nice and peaceful here and it's probably pretty much the way it appeared if you and I were standing in this very spot 200 years ago."

"It's called progress, Joe," the second surveyor said as he started walking down toward the water. "Not much we can do to stop it. I figure if we do the best job we can, well then at least everything they build will be where it's supposed to be."

"I guess you're right." Joe responded. "In fact, what I know about this particular company is that they always try to keep as much as they can of the natural attributes of the landsite. They just don't come in and tear out every tree and flatten the site." By now both men had made their way to the shoreline.

"This is where the marina will be." Joe said. "Looks like they'll have to dredge if they want to get any sailboats in here. And that old boatshed is probably going."

"Yeah, and I think there's going to be a small yard here with a ramp and a lift. I suspect most of these trees will have to go, don't you?" the second surveyor asked.

"Probably, but we have a lot to do before we start plotting this area."

The two men started their way back up the incline and began the task of surveying the overall construction site. This would keep them busy for the rest of the week.

*****

RJ sat at his desk at his firm's office in downtown Baltimore. He was busy signing some checks, what had become a daily part of the business by now. Today's stack was for various preliminary fees to cover initial planning and surveying of Phase I of Alder Cove and Marina. He was just finishing when engineering consultant, Frank Sanford, tapped lightly on the office door.

"Come on in, Frank. I need a break from this torture," RJ said as he motioned Sanford into the office.

"You maybe should keep that pen out because I'm afraid you will be writing some unexpected checks," Frank told him.

"And so it begins," RJ responded. "It happens on every project. It's called the 'Jesus-Christ-what-else-can-go-wrong?' phase. Okay, break the news gently, Frank."

"We had preliminary approval for the marina layout, but the county sent another guy out for a final look-see and he put the kibosh on a few things. Result is, we're not able to pull the permits we need, at least until we remedy the situation."

"Okay, Frank, I know you all too well." RJ responded. "I can tell by your quivering lip that the remedy for the situation isn't some minor detail. C'mon, out with it."

"Well the waterfront on the one side is pretty soft; softer than we anticipated and for a larger area than we first measured. There's more marsh there than we thought. So now, if we want to put the ramp and the lift on the upper side we have to provide some containment...meaning a seawall."

"What if we move the lift and the ramp to the other end?" George asked.

"Then we'd have sort of a domino effect. If we move the ramp and lift, we'll have to move the storage and shop facilities, and there isn't enough room for all that on that part of the property unless we take out a good five or six of those big oaks. We could do that, but since we promised we'd leave them in, the environmental folks would probably hang us from the last tree standing in addition to fighting the permits we need to construct the buildings. Sorry, RJ, but the best solution is the expensive one. We best put in a seawall. I recommend we run it the entire length of the water line. That will make it really safe and strong, plus it will look a lot better cosmetically."

"Did you discuss this with John yet?" RJ questioned, referring to John Manataglio, the architect on the project.

"Yeah, we both looked at it every which way before I drew short straw to come in here and tell you."

"Well, I'm not happy we misjudged our original survey. Not only does it cost us an unexpected expense, it will put us behind on the marina schedule," RJ said. "How long before we can clear the frontage and start on the wall?"

"Two to three weeks is our guess—if we hustle and the

county doesn't drag its heels." Frank responded. RJ stood up, hands in his pockets and stared down at the papers on his desk. Then he looked up at Frank.

"Okay then, let's hustle!"

*****

Louise Henderson shut the door to her house, stepped down the porch stairs and walked over to the driveway where her shiny new red Mustang was parked. She got in, revved the engine just enough to make a noisy impression on her neighbors, then pulled out and headed a few blocks up Liberty Street to Lawyers Row. She stopped in front of a small, colonial brick building, parked the car and went inside.

Bertram Randolph was a longtime friend of the Henderson family. But more so, he had been the bookkeeper and financial advisor to the family hardware business. That business had thrived for so many years partly due to Randolph's efforts. He had a keen sense of how to run the money part of a business, make it profitable and then put the profits where they would grow the most. Louise had no trust in anyone. The only exception was Bertram Randolph. She would follow any advice he offered to her, without question, despite his insistence that she understand everything he did for her.

Louise opened the outer door to the Randolph Accounting Firm and walked in. Bertram was getting a drink from the water cooler in the corner.

"Hi Uncle Bert," Louise called out cheerfully.

152

Randolph was not related to the Henderson family, but he had been such a close fixture for so many years that Sandra and Louise had always called him "Uncle." It suited him just fine, especially now that Louise had lost both her parents and he felt a responsibility to look after her. He was happy to see her sell the family business and make enough money to take care of herself for the rest of her life. He was, after all, in his 70's and knew he would not be able to watch over her much longer.

"So you're off your rocker again," Uncle Bert joked.

"Only because I wanted to come visit you," Louise replied. "I want your advice. I am thinking about selling the house. I know Mom and Dad would be very upset, but really, there is no one left in the family who wants to live there. RJ is off living across the bay in the big city and has his own life. Meanwhile, I'm all alone in this big house that I just don't want to have to take care of. Don't you think it makes sense, Uncle Bert?"

"Well, maybe you should think about keeping just the front porch and the rocker," he joked again, "since those are the parts you still use the most. But, no, I see no reason for you to live there by yourself. It's too much work and worry, unless... " he trailed off.

"Unless what?" Louise asked.

"Unless you think you may ever marry again. You know, it's not out of the question. You are still a very attractive lady and I know any number of men who would love to hear you say 'yes' to dinner and a movie."

"Not to worry, Uncle Bert," Louise assured him. "I have loved enough for one lifetime. The only two men I will have dinner with are you and RJ...and I don't need to be going to the movies afterwards."

"Well, then, sell the house if that makes you happy, but where will you go?"

"RJ keeps nagging me to look at the plans he has for his new development up the river. He says there will be some condominiums in addition to single homes. I just might take a look at the drawings and see what they're going to be like. I could probably get a very good deal; I've got connections, you know. Otherwise, I am sure I can find something smaller and trouble-free here in Centreville. I don't need much. As you say, a porch and rocker suit me just fine."

"In the meantime," Uncle Bert said, "my lawyer friend and I should have your new will finished this week. I just have to work on setting up the trusts you wanted for RJ's children. That won't take much longer. I'll call you when it's time to come sign."

"You're a prince, Uncle Bert," Louise responded and gave him a quick peck on the cheek and told him she'd be back when she had a buyer for the house. Then she left his office and zoomed off in her slick, cherry red Mustang.

As she often did, Louise would take a slight detour from where she was headed if she was anywhere near the World War II memorial the citizens had erected in a small park in downtown Centreville. Here, Louise would pull into a parking space, get out and walk up to the memorial. It appeared similar to many war memorials that stood in small towns and large cities across America. There was a large statue of a soldier atop a granite pedestal. On the front wall of the pedestal, engraved in a bronze plaque, were the names of the town's young men who gave their lives on some foreign soil or in oceans far far away from Sunday supper at their family dinner table.

As if routine, but she never considered it that, Louise would approach the bronze plaque, raise her hand and gently run her fingertips across the engraving of one man's name: Robert C. Harris.

CHAPTER 22

Donald D'Angelo woke up somewhat distressed and angry with himself. Within the past two days he had driven from Philadelphia to Rhode Island, and then spent all day hiking around several historic sites looking for clues that might help him solve the mystery of the dead letter his father retrieved from a mailroom on a U.S. Navy base during World War II. If anything by now, Donald was convinced he had made a bad decision. It was foolhardy to think that he would discover a forty-year-old tree stump at an almost randomly selected location in a state he had arbitrarily selected. And even if he had, what of it? He now thought that, in his passion for the hunt for some mystical treasure, he had probably relied on it being a storybook venture, one that would play itself out into some kind of great discovery and a happily-ever-after ending. Reality had hit him. He knew he would have to put a lot more thought and investigative skills to work if he were ever to solve the letter's secret. Luck, too, would have to be on his side.

He stopped off at the inn's restaurant for some breakfast. He was thinking about just going home, but he thought as long as he had come all this way he should at least spend some time in Coventry. He finished his breakfast, checked out of the inn, got in his car and proceeded north. It was not very far.

As he drove, Donald had given some thought as to what to do in Coventry. He knew there were two things that might provide some information. First, he thought he would go to the local Veterans of Foreign Wars and see if there was any local history of the town's men who had died in World War II. He thought if he was lucky, there may even be someone there who would remember who R was. That led him to his second idea. He would go to the local high school and see if there were any records there of students killed in the war. He took this one step further. He would ask if there were any teachers still around who taught at the school in the early 1940s. That was not so farfetched an idea. A teacher in her twenties at that time would now be in her sixties. If he could find such a person, maybe he or she would actually remember a student named Sandra and another whose named began with an "R," and that the two had fallen in love and he was killed in the war. "No, that's not so farfetched an idea," Donald thought.

When he got to Coventry, Donald stopped off at a coffee shop for a second cup and a look at the local phonebook. He wrote down the addresses of the VFW and the high school, got directions to both from the waitress and then off he went on what he hoped wouldn't turn out to be another wild goose chase. His first stop was the VFW. When he walked in there was an informal lobby area. In the center was a reception desk, but no one was there. A group of men were sitting at a table off to the side. They were playing cards.

"Can I help you?" one of the card players called out from across the room.

"I hope so," said Donald. "I'm looking for the name of a young man who was killed in World War II. He may have come from Coventry and all I know is that his first name begins with an 'R'."

The card player got up and walked over to Donald.

"Well, that could be Ralph, Roger Richard or Robert or whatever. Is that all you got, just 'R'?" the man asked.

"Yep, I know that's not much to go on, but it's all I got," Donald responded.

"My name is Alec," the man told Donald as he extended his hand. Donald shook his hand and introduced himself.

"Come on over here to this wall plaque," Alec said as he motioned Donald over. "It lists all the boys from Coventry who died in World War II. You can see if any had a first name with an 'R'."

Donald walked over and looked at the engraved names in the bronze plaque. He wrote down the names that began with an "R:" Ryan, Roger and Ricky. Just those three. He turned to Alec.

"Is there any more information available on these three names?" Donald asked.

"I guess if you have a date as to when they were killed, you could check the archives at the *Providence Journal*," the man told Donald. "They ran obituaries for just about every boy who lived in Rhode Island. If you don't have a date that could be one long search."

"That's an idea," Donald responded. But let me ask you a another question. Is there any local vet who you know that has a pretty good memory from back then and who may have known one of these three guys on the plaque whose name begins with 'R'?"

"Good idea," Alec said. "That'd be Fred Chambers," the man responded. He's our local walking encyclopedia of World War II."

"Do you know where I might find this Fred Chambers?" Donald asked.

"Across the room, guy playing cards on the left," Alec responded. Donald chuckled. Finally, some luck was showing itself in his treasure hunt.

"Well, then I hope he doesn't mind pausing the game for a minute," Donald said as he walked over to the man and introduced himself. Then he showed him the list of the three names.

"Did you know any of these guys and if they had a local girlfriend named Sandra who lived here?" Donald asked.

"I knew Ricky. We were in the same outfit, even went through boot together. He was killed on D-Day at Normandy. Shot before he ever made it ashore. His mother never got over it. But I don't remember any girl in his life. He was kind of shy and not very good looking, at least not the kind girls went for."

"Do you know if he still has any relatives or friends living nearby?" Donald asked.

"Don't think so," the Chambers told him. "His dad died last year and he didn't have any brothers or sisters. Now, this guy Ryan, he was from a big Irish family. But I doubt he had a girlfriend. He was going to be a priest. That's what he was about to do when he got drafted. He figured he'd just postpone that until he got back or somehow pursue it while he belonged to Uncle Sam in addition to God." Never happened, though. I guess God wanted him elsewhere because he and his whole crew went down somewhere over France if I remember right. Their plane was hit by ground fire and no one made it out." Donald scribbled all this down in his notebook as the Chambers was talking.

"And what about Roger?" Donald asked.

"Didn't know him. You'd have to do some research to find out his story," Fred Chambers replied.

Donald thanked the men and dropped a ten-dollar bill into the collection jar that sat atop the reception desk. He didn't think he had learned anything very helpful, except that he was confident that R was not for Ricky or Ryan, at least Ricky or Ryan from Coventry, Rhode Island. He got back in his car and headed over to the high school. Once there, he went into the school office just off to the side of the main entrance. There, he introduced himself to the woman sitting at the front desk. According to the nameplate on the desk, her name was Mrs. Carol Mason.

"Do you know if this is the same high school that served Coventry in the 1940s?" Donald asked.

"Well, it's not the same building and not the same staff, but it is still the same school," Mrs. Mason told him.

"I'm trying to research two students who may have gone to school here in the early 1940s. I have only the first name of a young lady and the first letter of the boy's first name. Are there lists of students that go back that far?" Donald inquired.

Mrs. Mason smiled. "You sound like that cartoon detective, Dick Tracy, my father used to read every day in the morning paper. Here you are coming in here trying to solve some big mystery and all you have is the first letter of a name," she said, laughing.

"I know, it's kind of crazy, but that's about all I have to go on." At this point a second woman approached the front desk. She had overheard most of the conversation.

"Sir, if there is a list, it's probably on microfiche and buried somewhere in the records department at the Board of Ed. I have a better idea. We have a copy of all the class yearbooks in our library here. If you want, you can have a seat here in the office and we'll get the years you want and you can go through them. They all have a list of graduates for each year."

"That would be fantastic," Donald told her. "I really appreciate your help." Donald was shown a seat at an empty table, and soon the yearbooks he requested arrived. He carefully went through each one. If he found a Sandra he would write her name down and then look for any "R" boys' names to match. He went through the yearbooks for 1940, 41, 42 and 43. When he was finished he had found two Sandras, one in 1941 and another in 1943. The 1941

161

Sandra had a matching Roger and Randolph on the boys' list. The 1943 Sandra had a matching Randall. Both Ryan and Ricky that he had learned about at the VFW showed up in the yearbook for 1942.

"Now what?" Donald thought to himself. He closed the yearbooks and arranged them in a stack. Then he approached Mrs. Mason again at the front desk.

"That was very helpful," he said, "I have a few full names now. But what I need is more information about them. Do you have any idea how I might go about locating a teacher from back then who is still living in Coventry today?"

"Let me call my mother," Mrs. Mason said.

"Do you have to ask permission or does your mother know someone?" Donald asked jokingly.

"My mother is the person you are looking for," Mrs. Mason told him. "She taught here back then and she has a memory like you wouldn't believe." With the phone at her ear, she motioned to Donald to wait a moment. He could not believe how much luck he was having. First the World War II vet who was right there playing cards at the VFW and now this lady's mother is exactly the person he is looking for.

"Hi Mom," Mrs. Mason said to the person on the other end of the phone. "We have a gentleman visiting the school today who is trying to find out some information about some students from back in the 1940s. He has some names and I thought maybe if you remember them you could tell him about them. Do you have time now to do that?" Mrs. Mason gave Donald a thumbs-up sign.

"Okay, I will put him on the phone and you two can reminisce all you want."

"My mother's name is Mildred," Mrs. Mason told Donald as she handed him the phone.

"Hello, Mildred. My name is Donald. I have an old letter that was written by a soldier in World War II. Parts of the letter are destroyed. I know that the young man's name began with an 'R' and the letter is addressed to a young woman named Sandra-something. I can tell from the letter they were probably in love with each other, maybe even engaged. He was killed in the Pacific shortly after he wrote the letter. That is about all I know about them. I looked at the yearbooks here at the school and there was a Sandra Gallagher in 1941 and a Sandra Hollander in 1943. Do you remember either of them and whether or not either had a boyfriend whose name began with an 'R'?"

"Sandra Gallagher I remember very well because her mother and I were good friends. She had a boyfriend in her senior year. He was on the football team; a boy named Ted something, but definitely Ted. They weren't together long. She met another boy right after high school. His name was Adam and that's whom she married a couple years later. He became a doctor and they moved to Boston. I guess they are still there. Not sure. Who was the other Sandra again?"

"Hollander, Sandra Hollander," Donald told her. "Does she ring a bell?"

"I'm not sure. There were two Hollanders. I think they may have been sisters. I do remember having both of them in my class at one time or another. The one that I think was Sandra was a tall thin girl. I don't recall any boys around her. Between you and me she was not very attractive."

Donald suddenly remembered another detail.

"Did Sandra's family own some kind of store, do you remember," he asked Mildred.

"Oh no, that I definitely remember. She was a farm girl. Sometimes came to school after doing some morning barn chores and you could tell. That's another reason she didn't attract any boys I suppose."

"Mildred, thank you so much for taking the time to talk to me," Donald told her.

"Sounds like I didn't help much. Neither one of them wound up with a boy whose name began with an 'R' that I can recall." Mildred said.

"No, but sometimes ruling some names out helps lead to the right one," Donald said. "So thanks very much." They each said goodbye, Donald thanked Mrs. Mason and left. He sat in his car for a few minutes wondering what to do. He was disappointed that he had not been able to at least discover one useful bit of information. He did, however, think his idea about talking to people at the VFW and the high school was a good one. Folks at both locations were able to remember names he came up with so that seemed to be a good tactic. He just hadn't come up with the right people at the right places yet.

Donald thought it would be best to cut his trip short and head home; there was nothing more he could do in Rhode Island. He was hungry, however, and it was late afternoon. He pulled into a roadside tavern near I-95. He'd grab a bite to eat and then drive home. He still had the next day off so he could sleep late the next morning.

The tavern had a soup and sandwich special that Donald saw a customer eating on the way in. That looked pretty good so that's what he ordered. He sat in a line of booths along the wall. Across from him was a typical neighborhood bar with a collection of neighborhood people sitting here and there. Directly across from him were three men who looked pretty weathered; boatmen of some type, Donald figured based on their appearance and the conversation they were having. There was a debate going on about which was the best season for stripers, spring or fall. Donald was all-city-boy; he had no idea what a striper was.

"Excuse me, gentlemen," Donald said, "I'm just curious. What's a striper?"

"That's a bass," all three of them answered in unison.

"Oh, I'm from Philly and I can tell you anything you want to know about a hoagie or a cheesesteak, but I don't know crap about fish," Donald said as he laughed a little. "Thanks for the education."

The three boaters continued their great debate. One man said spring was better because there were a lot more stripers. Another said fall was better because even though you had to be a lot more patient, the stripers you caught in the fall were so much larger. The conversation continued. The group argued bait, then line strength, then best time of day to fish. Then, they started telling their personal fish stories, each one's fish growing in size as the hour went on and the beer kept pouring.

As the men tested their debating skills, Donald had drifted away, his thoughts now totally embedded in his dead letter treasure hunt while he spooned his soup and chomped on a huge rare roast beef sandwich on a Kaiser. The voices of the three boaters chattered about in the background along with the sounds of dishes being washed, the beer tap being tapped and someone's favorite song playing on the jukebox every few minutes.

"...Y'know, Charlie," one of the trio was saying, "when you talk about that bad season a few years back that reminds me when I was a kid growing up on the Chesapeake and we'd have a bad year for jimmies That'd just about killed my daddy's business and that's what you were going through that year when..."

Donald suddenly stopped eating. Something jarred him. At first he wasn't sure, but then he realized what it was. He turned to the men on the bar stools next to him.

"Excuse me again," Donald said, "But did one of you just say something about jimmies?"

"Yeah I did," the man on the left said. "What about 'em?"

"What's a jimmie?" Donald asked.

"It's a blue crab; a large male Maryland blue crab. They're a big deal on the Chesapeake Bay. You've had blue crabs, ain't jah?" the man asked.

"Yeah, of course, but I never heard them called jimmies," Donald responded. He was ecstatic.

"Let me buy you guys a round," he said. "You just really gave me an education I can use!"

"Phil," yelled one of the boaters as he turned toward the

166

bartender, "this here man is buying us a round, so pour up and make one for him, too."

"Oh no, I'm okay, thanks," Donald said.

"What? You can't share a brew with a bunch of Rhode Island salts. We ain't good enough?"

"No, no," Donald said. "I'm over two years' sober and I'm not goin' back again; has nothing to do with you guys. You guys just made my day."

"Well that being the case," the man said as he turned back to the bartender, "Phil, pour this man a tall ginger ale so we can all toast the stripers in Rhode Island, the jimmies in Maryland and the hoagies in Pennsylvania."

Donald was halfway home and he was still floating inches above the car seat. He kept slapping the steering wheel, proclaiming, "I can't believe it. *Jimmies* God damn it. I can't believe it." He had come all the way to Rhode Island looking for answers to clues in the dead letter and found none...until luck would uncover one incredible piece of information: jimmies were crabs! Not just any crabs, but crabs from the Chesapeake Bay. His trip to Rhode Island was successful after all. He now knew for sure the letter from R to Sandra was originally destined for Maryland.

CHAPTER 23

Donald took advantage of his final day off. He slept late. Despite the excitement he had after discovering Maryland was the state he was looking for, it was a long drive home and he was both physically and mentally exhausted when he finally drove into his driveway and parked the car. He went inside and to bed almost immediately. He awoke around eleven the next morning. He decided he would go out for some breakfast and then come back and begin studying his map of Maryland and the Chesapeake Bay. He would spend several hours sitting at the kitchen table, searching for Maryland towns beginning with the letter "C." It wasn't long before Donald had the names of 18 towns on his list. He was relieved that Maryland was a lot closer to Philadelphia than Rhode Island, but there was no way he could easily drive to eighteen towns.

Donald began to narrow the list. He would eliminate any town that was not directly on a river near the Chesapeake Bay. There were some towns on the Bay itself, another on a canal, but R's letter specifically referred to a river so he was going to stick with that criterion.

By late afternoon he had shortened the list to five towns: Cambridge, Centreville, Charlestown, Chestertown and Church Creek. Even five was too many. But the trip to Rhode Island continued to reveal more accurate methods of research than merely walking around looking for tree stumps. Donald had had some success when he spoke with the vets and again with people at the high school. While he did not get any good leads, he definitely got names and other information that were helpful in the process of elimination. So, he thought, he would continue his search by contacting the VFW branch and the high school for each of the five towns. If he didn't actually discover the home of R and Sandra, at least he would possibly be able to say where they did not live.

The day had slipped away while Donald sat at the map of Maryland on his kitchen table. By now, he felt it was probably too late to make calls to anyone. He would, however, attempt to get a list of phone numbers for all the places he wanted to contact. And that's how he spent his evening, on the phone with directory assistance tracking down all the telephone numbers he needed.

The next morning it was back to the bookstore. Donald was sorry that he hadn't taken a few more days' vacation. He thought he was hot on the trail of solving the dead letter puzzle and he was so focused on that; anything else was an interruption—especially opening several boxes of new books and having to set up their display shelves. He would have to wait until his lunch break to squeeze in some of the calls he wanted to make.

*****

What was to become a dazzling new home and marina development on the Eastern Shore, was now nothing more than several acres of fenced-in land overgrown with tall grass, years of unrestrained spreading shrubbery and an endless assortment of grown trees. The chain-link fence extended all along the access road, then turned inward and ran across fields and through dense wooded areas until ending at the shoreline along the Alder Branch, just off the Corsica River. Within the confines of this fence, homesites would soon be plotted and cement foundations poured. Along with individual homes, there would be "garden-rise" condominiums and townhomes. Everything possible would be done to leave as much of the natural environment and the more "sacred" trees undisturbed. The developer had a life-long respect for the Chesapeake Bay and its surrounding territory. It was his passion to build a development that would blend in with this unique environment; a development he knew his mother and father would have admired.

This morning was drizzly. The rain fell gently on the tin roof of the boatshed that fit snuggly inside a small grove of trees along the shoreline of the new construction site for Alder Cove and Marina. A dredging barge was anchored in the shallow water just a few feet away. Soon, it would begin sucking out the muddy bottom along the new property line and then dredge a channel out to the middle of the Alder Branch. Eventually, residents of Alder Cove could motor through the new channel and tie up their sloops and motor yachts to the new piers at the community's marina. But first, the dredging and construction of a new seawall. Things were beginning to take shape. The boatshed, rustically poised in its place for probably half a century, would soon be pushed and pulled aside unceremoniously by the huge blade of a backhoe.

RJ Henderson was very busy these days. As president and owner of the company that was building Alder Cove and Marina, his days were filled with frantic phone calls, purchase orders and payroll checks, architectural drawings and countless people interrupting every moment. Such was the atmosphere of developing a large residential community.

RJ thrived in the midst of all this activity. He so looked forward to opening day and the pride he would feel for his accomplishment. He had broken the cycle of the Eastern Shore by escaping its stronghold and building his life outside its confines. But here he returned to build a magnificent community in a gesture dedicated to showing his gratitude to his mother for making it all happen.

RJ was well aware that he selected a site along the Alder Branch because his mother had lost her life in its waters. He viewed it as a happy memorial in what otherwise was a tragic location. Somehow he sensed that his mother actually had a reason for being in the Alder that evening despite years of avoiding it whenever he was with her. At the time of her death, he went numb. He felt little need to know the details and, in fact, didn't want to hear them. He had enough pain. He did not want to compound it by second guessing all the what-ifs that more information would have speculated. That she died in the Alder was enough. It was such a peaceful body of water and he envisioned her passing to be surreally peaceful. He did not want to disrupt that impression with any other information that would paint a different picture. Hence, RJ had no idea that his mother's boat had been tied up at the very same boatshed that was about to be demolished to make way for his new marina. He knew nothing about the role it played in the life of his parents when they were young and so much in love. It was almost as if fate had drawn him to this precise location on which to build his community. He simply had no idea of its significance.

CHAPTER 24

Donald's telephone marathon with the five Maryland towns was not progressing as quickly as he would have liked. The calls had to be made during business hours if he had any chance of connecting with anyone. This was precisely the time of day that least afforded any opportunity for him to make personal phone calls. He had left quite a few messages and was awaiting callbacks. Some came when he was either out of the store or waiting on a customers and unable to take the call. So, much of the procedure was hit or miss. He did, however, manage to rule out Church Creek and Charlestown. Neither of these towns had a soldier whose first name began with the letter "R" listed on its World War II memorial plaque.

It was Thursday and he had been at it all week. Making calls whenever he had a few moments free, or taking callbacks when he could. He had packed a sandwich for lunch every day so he could take his lunch break in the back office and hopefully make a few more calls. He had called the VFW Post in Centreville several times and got only a recording. Today he tried again. With his mouth half-full of a bite from a ham and cheese on rye, the number he dialed began to ring. It was answered almost immediately. Donald swallowed quickly.

"Hello, Centreville VFW," a voice answered. It was an elderly voice, a little wheezy and slow.

"Hello, my name is Donald D'Angelo and I am calling from Philadelphia. I am trying to locate the home of a soldier who died in World War II and he may have lived in your town. I don't have much information about him, but do you think you may be able to take a minute to help me?" Donald asked.

"Well, I can tell you this," responded the elderly voice, "I'm a World War II vet and this is my hometown and I probably knew most of the boys from here who fought in the war. It's not a big town, even smaller back then. Most everybody knows everybody. What information do you have?"

"Not much," Donald said. "His first name began with an "R" and the chances are pretty good that he was killed at Tarawa in 1943. I also know that--"

"That'd be Robert Harris," the man said interrupting Donald in mid-sentence.

"Robert Harris. You know who it was that quickly?" Donald asked.

"Yep, he and I were both hometown boys here, went through school together. We weren't friends, but, like I said, everybody knew everybody. Funny story about Robert and me. I once sat in a seat next to his girlfriend. He paid me a buck to give it up so he could sit there. What he didn't know was that I only sat there for a minute to tie my shoelace. I was about to get up and go sit near the window, but I took the buck anyway." The elderly voice laughed out loud.

"That girlfriend...would she happen to be named Sandra?" Donald asked.

"Sandra Henderson. She and Robert were inseparable."

Donald found himself so excited he began to stutter.

"Ah-and her fa-father owned a store of some kind?" Donald continued questioning, his heart now racing, letting him know how startled he was to realize he had finally located R and Sandra.

"Centreville Hardware. It was huge. One of the biggest businesses in town. Robert probably would have wound up owning it if he hadn't died in the war. So does all this answer your questions?" the elderly man asked.

"Where's Sandra now.   Does she still live in Centreville?"

"No, she died a few years ago. Tragic. Drowned in the river. No one knows how. Her sister still lives here." the man told Donald.

"Really! That's good news. What's her name? Do you know how I might get in touch with her?"

"Her name is Louise Henderson. She went back to using her maiden name after she and her husband split. I'll tell you what," the man said, "You give me your name and phone number and I'll see that she gets it."

"Okay, but please tell her I have something, a letter from Robert to Sandra that he wrote just before he was killed. It was never delivered because the envelope was destroyed. She may want to see it. Will you tell her that for me, please?" Donald asked.

"Yes, I'll do that. I bet she would like to see that."

Donald gave the man his phone number for the bookstore and the one at home. He told the man that Louise should call him as soon as possible, even in the middle of the night. They hung up. Donald leaped out of his seat. The adrenaline was pumping his heart overtime and his emotions were on runaway mode.

"Yes! We did it, Pop! We did it! It's no longer a dead letter—it's alive! You and I solved the puzzle!"

Donald could hardly contain himself and working the rest of the afternoon was the last thing he wanted to do. Every time the phone rang he jumped up and nervously waited to see if it was Louise Henderson. When it was time to go home he was afraid to leave. He didn't want to miss her call. He drove home in record time. As he walked into the house the phone was ringing. He ran to answer it.

"Hello," he almost yelled into the receiver.

"Hello, is this Mr. D'Angelo?" a woman's voice asked on the other end.

"Yes, this is Donald D'Angelo. Is this Louise Henderson?"

"Yes, this is Louise. I understand you have an old letter that was written to my sister. Is that right?" Louise asked.

"Yes, yes, I do. It is a long story and I would love to tell you about it. Do you have time now?" Donald asked.

"Yes I do. I have all the time in the world these days,"

"Well, good, Miss Hender—ah, may I call you Louise?" Donald asked.

"Yes, of course and I assume I may call you Donald?" she responded.

Donald and Louise would spend the next half-hour on the phone together. Donald explained what a dead letter was and how his father had brought Robert's letter back from San Diego after the war and how his father had tried for a long time to find out where it was supposed to go. He told her how he had been searching non-stop since he found it in his father's box of old Navy stuff. He explained why he decided to go to Rhode Island and how it was there that he actually learned about *jimmies*—the ultimate clue that directed him to Maryland.

Louise told Donald how her sister and Robert were the town's sweethearts and how everyone knew they would be married the minute he returned from the war...but that was never to happen. She told him about RJ and what a miracle Sandra considered her son to be and how she devoted her life to his success. Then she asked Donald if he would read the letter to her over the phone. Donald paused.

"Well, Louise," he began to tell her, "I'm not sure I want to do that. I will not keep it from you, no no. I won't do that. But it contains a mystery, sort of a puzzle that Sandra had to solve. Robert gave her clues and told her she would find some kind of treasure he had left for her. I feel at this point I have an investment in this letter. My father and I have spent countless hours trying to decipher where it was supposed to go and to whom. I think you and I need to meet and have some understanding about this treasure."

"Oh, all this does seem so mysterious," Louise said. "I will not deny you have devoted yourself to solving the puzzle of the letter, but I will need to see it before we can discuss anything further."

"I can meet you early Saturday morning. I'll drive down and you can see the letter and then maybe we can both figure out what is fair. Is that okay?" Donald asked.

"That sounds fine. What time do you think you will be here?" asked Louise.

Donald explained he would get an early start and be there by 9 o'clock Saturday morning. He told her if she were able to identify any of the clues in the letter, it might just be possible they'd be going on a treasure hunt!

CHAPTER 25

Ray Hanson had just finished supervising the off-loading and placement of the office trailer at the construction site for Alder Cove and Marina. This rectangular metal and wood box would be his and RJ's home for the next year and more. Shortly after the truck that brought it left, two more trucks arrived, large flatbed trucks. One carried a huge bulldozer and the other a backhoe. These, too, were off-loaded and the equipment made ready to go.

Ray, a longtime friend and colleague of RJ's, was the foreman on site. Permits were finally in hand and work on the waterfront could begin. The initial schedule called for six-day work weeks, Monday through Saturday. The first task would be getting the seawall in place. Work on the marina would start soon after.

Today, the bulldozer would begin clearing the shoreline and the backhoe would start tugging at the old dock and boatshed as soon as it had access. Ray expected to get a lot done today. He was on a tight deadline.

*****

Donald D'Angelo was up early Saturday morning and on his way to the Eastern Shore of Maryland before sunrise. This time he headed south on I-95 and after going through the Harbor Tunnel at Baltimore, he switched over to I-97, then onto Route 50 to the Chesapeake Bay Bridge just north of Annapolis. Once across the bridge it was a short drive back north to Centreville.

When he pulled into the driveway in front of the old Henderson home, Louise sat gently rocking on the front porch. Seated next to her was Uncle Bert. She wanted him handy just because she was a little unsure about this man from Philadelphia who claimed to have a 40-year-old letter for her sister. Donald got out of the car.

"Good morning," he said as he approached the porch steps.

"'Morning, Donald. This here is my sidekick, Uncle Bert. I asked him to join us today. I bet you'd like some coffee," Louise said, welcoming Donald.

"You bet I would. I was up just a bit early this morning, but the drive was beautiful, especially coming over the Bay Bridge." Louise was getting up.

"It certainly is a sight, whether you're going over or under it," she said. "You can sit here and small talk with Uncle Bert and I'll go get us all some coffee."

Donald shook Bert's hand and sat down in the chair

180

next to him. They talked about the weather and a trip to Annapolis Donald had made the year before. Soon, Louise returned with a large tray of coffee and an array of pastries.

"Wow, this was well worth the trip. Thank you, Louise," Donald said.

"Help yourselves, boys," Louise said as she sat back down in her rocker. She told Donald she had explained to Uncle Bert about the dead letter and the long search Donald and his father had undertaken to find its owner.

"I am impressed by the effort you and your father made to get this letter delivered after all these years," Bert told him, "I probably would have given up long ago."

"Well," Donald responded, "there is some motivation, as you will see when you read the letter, but I admit just trying to solve the puzzle was interesting enough. My father and I always liked a good mystery story."

Donald poured a cup of coffee and grabbed a blueberry Danish and set them on the small table next to his chair. Then, he unzipped the leather case he had on his lap and pulled out Robert's letter, still neatly preserved in the plastic pocket. He handed it to Louise.

"I have long wished I would be handing this directly to Sandra," Donald told her, "but being as she is no longer with us, I suppose it now belongs to you and I am very pleased to deliver this piece of mail—finally—to its rightful owner."

Louise reached out and took the letter. She put on a pair of glasses and began reading it to herself. It was not long before her eyes moistened and a single tear formed and trailed off down her cheek. She wiped at it with a napkin. When she finished, she looked up at Donald.

"It is somewhat puzzling—not the meaning of the clues he writes about, but the whole attitude of the letter is quite strange. I cannot tell if it is a deep emotional love letter, or a letter that is somehow saying he is upset and bidding my sister goodbye. It makes no sense. She removed her glasses as she handed the letter to Uncle Bert and he took a minute or two to read it before handing it back to her.

"I see your point. Knowing how madly in love the two of them were, he says some strange things that I don't understand," Bert said.

"Can I ask that you read it aloud so we can go through it sentence-by-sentence so that I have some understanding of what Robert is trying to tell her?" Donald asked.

"Certainly," Louise responded. "Some of it is quite simple for me to figure out. You see, Sandra and I were very close, especially when we reached that age where all we did was gossip about the boys in our lives. Except she just had one boy in her life, while I had a different one every week. There wasn't much we did not know about each other...or about the boys we each had an interest in. She and Robert got serious in high school and there was never any doubt they'd get married as soon as he returned from the war. The day he left broke her heart, but she was determined to support him with all her heart as she waited for him to come home from the war. When we got word that he had been killed, it was shocking. He had been gone only a few months. It was all too sudden. Sandra was devastated. She was never the same after that day. She stayed alone in her room for the longest time. She wouldn't even let me in. Then one day she came out, announced she was pregnant with Robert's baby. After that all hell broke loose. She was as determined as anyone I'd ever seen to make sure her son was given every opportunity possible.

She couldn't have cared less about what folks might have thought about her being pregnant out of wedlock. She considered the baby a gift from God, like it was meant to make up for Robert being killed. Seems the rest of the town took it the same way. I never heard of one person ever saying anything negative about the situation. And RJ—ah, that was her son—well, he was just like his dad. Before long everybody just sort of adopted him and went out of their way to see he got anything he needed.

Sandra, meanwhile, literally poured herself into the family hardware business. It wasn't long before she knew more about hardware and tools and construction stuff than any man in town. And being as she was such a beautiful lady, she always had a swarm of men buzzin' around her. But she had no interest. The store and her son were her total focus until the day she died.

So, anyway, that's just to give you some background. My sister was a wonderful person. Now, let's see what we can figure out with this letter."

Louise took a sip of coffee, put her glasses back on and began reading aloud.

Dear Sandra,
So much has changed since my last day at home that I hardly think I am the same person. In fact, I <u>know</u> I am not the same person you once knew. I have so many fond memories

of our little rural town—our farm, my parents and friends,
Eddie and Uncle Tim and, of course, you.

Louise paused and then looked up to explain.

"The farm was Robert's parents' farm. It was just a couple of miles outside of town. It had been in his family for generations. His folks got old and weren't able to take care of it anymore and since Robert was gone, there was no one to inherit it. So his father sold it off in parcels to some of his neighbors. Eddie was Robert's cousin. Eddie's mother had died in childbirth having a second baby a couple of years after Eddie was born. His father—that's Uncle Tim—was a waterman so he was gone a lot of the time. Eddie wound up living with Robert and his parents. He was the same age as Robert. Eddie and he both signed up together to join the Marines and on the day they were supposed to leave for training camp, Eddie was nowhere to be found. He was always sort of a loner and we all figured he just got cold feet at the last minute and took off. We never saw him after that and nobody knows where he lives today." Louise went back to reading more of the letter.

I saw you standing in the window of your father's store
when we were pulling out. Oh that I could erase what has
happened and bring all the good times back, I would. But
now I have traveled clear across the country from the
Atlantic to the Pacific and my ticket is not marked for a
return trip.

Louise paused to comment.

"Sandra didn't want to see him leave, but at the last minute she went to the store and tried to hide herself behind a sign in the window as she watched his bus go down the street. I was with her. We were both crying like babies. I don't know what he means about *erasing what has happened,* except maybe he means his joining the Marines and going off to war." Louise returned to the letter.

I have new friends now—my brothers in the Marines. We all look out for each other. At this moment we are at sea and there is the cold reality that many of us, including me, may not be here on this good earth much longer. I have accepted my mortality and actually think it may be the only way to end the misery I find occupying me body and soul. How I wish that it were different. How I wish that it has not become so difficult for me to want to survive and return to you.

Louise read the last sentence twice.

"Here is where it starts to get confusing. I don't know what he means by any of this. Why would it have been difficult for him to want to survive? Maybe something happened. This all just doesn't make any sense to me."

My only recourse to all my horror is revenge. It is my temperament, you know that. It will be the only thing that lives on after I die. You must accept it and know that I loved you more than anything in the world, ever, and that losing you was the one thing I would not accept.

"More gibberish," Louise said. "Maybe he had seen some badly wounded soldiers and he wanted to revenge their injuries. By 'my temperament' he means his quick temper I'm sure. He could be hot-headed if he wanted to be."

And so, my dearest Sandra, since it is unlikely we shall ever be together again, I have left you a treasure—a treasure you valued more than me. It is a priceless token of my devotion to you and what length I would go to, to mourn the end of our love. War is just not here before me in this strange part of the world. It was there, too, on the banks of the beautiful river I loved, disguised so I would never see it coming. Just as the enemy here is disguised. But the enemy here knows I am coming. And like the one at home, the one here will destroy me, too.

"Wow. This all just throws me for a loop. I cannot think of anything that Sandra valued more than Robert. The 'river' is the Corsica, of course. Anybody who is born and raised around here spends half their life on the river. But what this enemy at home is all about, I haven't the slightest idea."

Go now and look for your treasure. It will make everything clear. It will put an ending on the story. It will free you from not knowing and not wanting. Rev up Uncle Tim's old motor like I taught you and travel the roads we took to our majestic castle. But leave the net behind and take a shovel instead. You'll not be capturing jimmies this day. Find the tree along the back side, the one we cut to remember our magical day. On the opposite side, just a foot or two away, begin your dig and take, my love, what I have left for you.

186

"Okay, here is where things start making sense. Uncle Tim's motor was the one on his skiff. Robert and Sandra would take his uncle's skiff out on the river all the time. They were on that skiff more than they were in his truck. They both loved to go crabbing and just spending the day on the river. The motor was really tricky to start and Sandra used to always brag how Robert had figured out how to get it going better than even Uncle Tim. He taught her the secret."

Louise paused and took another sip of coffee.

Travel the roads we took to our majestic castle.

"That means take the river to the castle. The castle was a figure of speech. It was this old dilapidated boatshed that was up the Alder Branch which is a small tributary a little ways up the river from Centreville. They used to call it their castle. It was their romantic hideaway. They'd go there a lot just to be alone and talk and whatever. They would do a lot a crabbing there, too. And, based on what they always came home with, it was a pretty good spot for crabs.

"My God," said Donald, "And here I was searching all over Rhode Island looking for a real castle and it turns out to be, what did you say, a *boatshed*?"

"A boatshed," said Louise. "They're like a garage, but built for your boat and they're right on the shoreline in the water so you can pull your boat inside and protect it."

"I wished I had known that a month ago," Donald said, laughing. Louise continued.

"This stuff about a shovel and leaving a net behind and no jimmies….he obviously means a crabbing net. Jimmies, as you've discovered, Donald, are large male crabs, the ones you really want lots of. The shovel I guess is for digging up whatever he left for it her."

The tree we cut...

"Well, Louise told me he carved their initials in a tree behind the boatshed so I am sure that is what he means by that. My, this is all pretty exciting, Donald. I can see why you got the bug for a treasure hunt." Louise went back to reading the final part of the letter.

It will be difficult, given what I know now, to force myself to forget it all and make our last day together, when we ran wild in the rain, the final memory I will be holding onto when the last breath escapes my body and sets me free from all that has happened.

"This is still more of the same," Louise said. "The same as all the other parts I don't quite understand. Maybe the treasure will explain what he means. We will have to go look for it if we can."

"Do you know where this boatshed is?" Donald asked Louise.

"She would never go up the Alder after Robert died. She has told me all about the place so I was pretty curious. One day when we were out on the river together we went by it and I asked her to go into the Alder and show me the

188

boatshed. She refused at first, but I really pleaded with her. She turned the boat that way and up the Alder we went. We didn't have to go far. There, tucked away inside a little cove was this old boatshed. It wasn't too romantic looking to me, but I didn't say that to her. She just started tearing up badly and told me we couldn't stay; she had to go."

"So you could take us there?" Donald asked.

"That was some 25-30 years ago. It may be long gone, no trace of it left at all. I have no idea how to get there by car and, besides, I doubt there is a road that even takes you there. We'd have to go by boat."

"Is it possible we could do that today? I'd gladly rent a boat if we can." Donald told her.

"Getting a boat probably isn't a problem. My neighbor, Jake, might take us in his. But I suppose we have to have some understanding about this treasure before we go," Louise said. "Robert was just a poor farm boy and I doubt very much he had anything of great value. I think whatever he left Sandra was some kind of token of his devotion, some sentimental thing she would cherish. That being the case, I wouldn't have much objection to sharing its value. I may want to keep it, but whatever its value is, we could split that. Is that fair?" she asked Donald.

"That sounds fair to me," Donald responded.

"Uncle Bert, what do you think?" Louise asked as she turned to Bert.

"I agree," Bert said, "I don't think there is anything of value to be found. But even so, if you both are willing to agree to split it evenly between you, that sounds like a good idea. Louise, why don't you go see if Jake can take you and

I'll go inside and write up a little agreement you both can sign and Jake and I can witness it. Nothing long and too lawyer-like, but just enough to spell out that you two have an agreement."

"That'd be great," Donald told him. Louise agreed. She went next door and roused Jake out of his easy chair and asked him if he would take her and Donald up the river for a short trip in his boat. He said yes.

Uncle Bert wrote out two identical documents and had everyone sign them. He gave Louise and Donald each a copy.

"Okay, there you go," Bert told them. "Happy treasure hunting. Louise, call me when you get back and let me know how it all turned out."

"Oh, can't you join us?" Donald asked.

"No thanks. I'm getting a little too old to be out in a boat. I can just about balance myself on the sidewalk, let alone on a wobbly boat. You two have fun, but I'll be anxious to hear your story when you get back," Bert said.

CHAPTER 26

The bulldozer, with its engine idling, sat parked on the ridge just above the shoreline along the new Alder Cove and Marina construction site. Its diesel engine's rhythmic breathing drowned out the usual peaceful sound of chirping birds in the treetops. The hinged cap atop the exhaust stack rattled in the escaping gases, occasionally slapping down onto the pipe when the engine sputtered and lost a beat. This motorized symphony would be an ongoing concert for several days as trees were toppled and earthen mounds were flattened to level perfection. Squirrels, field mice, rabbits and hundreds of other little creatures would suddenly find their homesteads in upheaval as they panicked to escape the giant rolling metal plates of the tractor treads descending upon them from the huge yellow, smoke-breathing monster above.

Foreman Ray Hanson was busy taking pictures this day. Photography was his hobby and he always documented the sites he worked on, from clearing day to the ribbon-cutting ceremony. It was lunchtime and the men who had been working the bulldozer and backhoe sat under a shady tree, lunch pails open and various foil-wrapped packages strewn around them.

"Are we going to get to the dock and boatshed today?" Ray asked.

"About another hour or two and you can kiss them goodbye," the one worker responded.

"Well, give me a squawk on the walkie-talkie before you do it. I want to watch it go." Ray said.

"Will do, Ray," the worker told him just as Ray snapped his picture, catching the man's jaws closing down on an oversized turkey sandwich.

*****

Jake Tasker, Louise's neighbor, put the key in the ignition of his 16-foot bowrider and started the engine. Donald, meanwhile, grabbed hold of Louise's arm as she stepped off the dock and into the boat.

"It's been awhile since I've been out," she said. "I'll have to get my sea legs back, assuming they are willing to make the return trip," she said jokingly.

"Well, being a city boy," Donald joked, "I don't think I'll try the water skis this trip." After Louise was situated, he went back onto the dock and loaded an ice chest onto the boat. Lunch and drinks were inside. He also stowed the shovel that he got out of the back seat of his car. Louise leaned over and uncleated the stern line as Jake did the same to the bow. A slight push off the dock as Jake put the engine in gear and the treasure hunt was underway.

While the morning had been bright and sunny, by noon the clouds were tumbling in over the river and the day had gone from bright yellow to dreary gray. Jake held the boat at a moderate speed, not wanting to jar his guests more than necessary. It was not a long trip to the Alder Branch. As Jake turned the boat to starboard he cut the engine speed and proceeded slowly.

"It's low tide," Jake said. "We'll have to take it slow because I'm not too familiar with the water back in here."

"We don't have far to go if I remember right and IF the darn shed is still there." Louise yelled back at him. She and Donald had moved up to the bow of the boat and began scanning the shoreline for the boatshed. The boat cruised slowly as it peeked around the outgrowth of several trees bunched together in a small cove. There, set back along the marshy shore, the edge of a structure slowly began to appear.

"My God, there it is!" Louise yelled. "I can't believe it is still there!" She was on her feet, holding onto the bow rail with one hand and pointing with the other.

Jake steered the boat into the cove, ever so slowly, still being cautious, not wanting to run aground. As the boatshed came into full view, so too did a large construction machine, its huge claw-like appendage arched high in the air just above the roof of the boatshed. The motor on the monstrous vehicle came to life and a cloud of black smoke puffed out of its stack and the engine coughed up a loud backfire. The huge clawed bucket began to stir, slowly reaching out and over the entire roof of the boat shed. Donald could not believe what he was seeing.

"They're going to tear it down!" he yelled. Louise was flailing her arms back and forth in the air and yelling.

"Stop! Stop! Don't touch that boatshed," she screamed. Jake sped up the boat a little and pointed the bow directly toward the small dock surrounding the shed. The three of them were all shouting at the workman seated in the small cabin atop the chugging machine.

The noise of the backhoe was much louder and no one on shore heard the shouts from the three people just offshore in a small boat. It was only because the driver of the backhoe turned his head slightly to flick his cigarette butt out into the water that he caught sight of the boat. He did not quite know what to make of the three people frantically waving and yelling at him. He did, however, turn off the backhoe's engine so he could hear.

By now Jake had maneuvered the boat up to the dock and Donald had jumped up onto it and was running frantically toward the backhoe.

"You gotta stop," he yelled. "You can't tear down that shed!" Louise was on his heels, still yelling at the top of her lungs.

"What the hell?" was all the backhoe operator could say. By now, Ray Hanson, who was standing and watching from up on the ridge above the shoreline, was down and walking out onto the dock.

"What's the matter?" he asked the strangers, both of whom were out of breath and looking a bit disheveled by now.

"You can't tear down that boatshed just yet," Donald

told him. "We've got to take a look around for a few minutes. There may be something hidden here and we've come to find it."

"Well I'm not sure I have the authority to stop work on this site. We're on a tight schedule and you're on private property," Ray told them.

"Please," Louise said, "just give us a little time to look for something."

"This all is beyond me. The boss is up in the office. I'll have to get him down here and you can talk with him," Ray told Louise as he pulled the walkie-talkie from its leather case attached to his belt.

"RJ, you there?" Jack said into the walkie-talkie.

"RJ!" Louise yelled. "Is this RJ's Alder Cove? RJ Henderson?"

"Yeah, Ray whatcha need?" RJ called back on the walkie-talkie. Louise was in Ray's face by now.

"You tell RJ that his Aunt Louise is down here on the dock and needs to see him right away," she yelled at Ray.

Ray was perplexed. He pushed the button on the walkie-talkie.

"Ah, RJ, we have a little problem at the boatshed. There are some folks down here asking us not to tear it down. One of them is a lady who says she's your Aunt Louise and she's insisting you come down here." Ray explained.

"Aunt Louise?" Ray asked. "Louise, my Aunt Louise? Are you kidding?"

Louise grabbed the walkie-talkie out of Ray's hands and pushed the button.

"Yes, RJ it's Aunt Louise. You have to come down here

right this minute."

"What the hell—ah, okay, I'm on my way."

Within a minute or two a white pickup truck with a big Corsica Development logo on the door pulled up on the ridge overlooking the boatshed. The door opened and out stepped RJ. He made his way down the slope and onto the dock.

"Aunt Louise, what are you doing here?" RJ asked.

"I can't believe this is the location you picked for your development. I never really gave it much thought, but now it all makes sense. This is just too much to believe," Louise said. She was exasperated and breathing heavily by now. There was a step up at the end of the dock. Donald took Louise by the arm.

"Come Louise," he told her. "Sit down on this step. Jake, can you get her something to drink from the ice chest?"

He led Louise to the step and she sat down. When Jake arrived with the drink, she took a few sips and seemed to have gotten her breath back.

"I suppose we should all take a moment and tell each other what this is all about," RJ suggested. Louise took another sip.

"I'm okay now," she said. "I'm not used to this much excitement. My excitement days are supposed to be over. RJ, this gentleman is Donald D'Angelo. He came down from Philadelphia today to visit me. His father, back in World War II, worked in the mail system for the military and he got hold of a letter your father wrote to your mother just before he was killed. The envelope was destroyed and

Donald's father tried to figure out who the letter was supposed to go to or at least who wrote it. He worked on it for a long time. Eventually, Donald found the letter in his father's papers after his father died. Donald then took up the cause and has been trying to find out who was supposed to get the letter." Louise was still a bit winded. Donald continued the story.

"The letter has clues in it that my father and I have been trying to solve," Donald explained. "The clues were meant for your mother to help her find something that your father left behind for her. After I finally located Louise, she was able to explain all the clues in the letter because, as you know, your mother and her knew everything about each other."

"Well, that's really fascinating and I can't wait to see the letter," RJ said, "but what does all this have to do with that boatshed?"

"Sit, RJ because my neck is getting cramped looking up at you," Louise said as she massaged the back of her neck. RJ sat down on the dock. Louise looked him in the eyes.

"The boatshed was your mother and father's sanctuary. It was their castle, as they used to call it. They would come here often, just to be by themselves. They loved being on the river. They loved going crabbing together. And they loved this place. It was here where they could be alone and in love and no one else ever knew about it. You did not want to know the details of your mother's death and even if you do not believe in fate, you have to stop and wonder how come this place is where you chose to build your dream. This very place, this cove, RJ, is where you were conceived. It was the one and only time your mother and father ever strayed. But, perhaps fate played a hand. It was on the eve of your father's leaving for training camp. I think they sensed they may never have the opportunity again. And when you came along, your mother took you as a gift, a gift left behind to ensure your parents' love would endure.

So, RJ, this is not some random location. And it was here where your mother came the night she died. She came here deliberately. She had completed her mission in life. You had escaped the Eastern Shore, just as your father had hoped to do. You were the first Henderson to go to college. You were becoming a success. Her work was done. She returned here to be with Robert. She tied her boat up in the shed just as they always had. She took her clothes off and folded them neatly on the dock. And, as she and your father did on that wonderful night before he left, she went skinny dipping in the river. Here is where she was at rest and here is where she had been most happy. I do not know exactly how she died, but I do believe it was intentional, it was peaceful and with love in her heart. So, RJ, if this development of yours is meant to be a tribute to your mother and father, it is at the precise location it is meant to be. And, RJ...you cannot tear down their castle."

There was a long silence. No one spoke for what seemed minutes. Even the tough construction workers appeared captivated by the story.

"And so I won't," RJ said. "I won't tear it down. In fact, we will stop everything and redesign the waterfront. We can take the boatshed and shore it up structurally but keep its rustic beauty. You are right, Aunt Louise, it cannot be destroyed. And, I think fate may have had something to do with your arriving here just moments before that backhoe would have done its job."

"Okay, enough with all these tears," Louise said. Your father is sending us on a treasure hunt. Donald, get the shovel. Back there, somewhere, is a tree with Sandra and Robert's initials carved in it."

Everyone scattered, inspecting every tree that surrounded the boatshed. Donald went back to the boat to get the shovel. Ray found the tree almost immediately.

"Over here," he yelled. "Here it is." Indeed, there it was, a carving still deeply cut into the trunk of a large Sassafras tree with the aged, encrusted initials, "RH+SH – 7-24-43." Louise put her hand up to the tree and gently rubbed the crude engraving.

"Forty years. So long ago," she said, "yet it seems like just a little while. It is all exactly as she described."

Donald walked to the other side of the tree and started digging. Ray took the shovel from him.

"Here, let me do that, I'm used to it." he said. Donald thanked him as they all stood anxiously around the base of the Sassafras. Ray dug a good foot or more down into the soft ground. Slowly there appeared a sheet of some kind of material. It looked like an old disintegrated shower curtain. There were shells and seahorses faintly printed on it. Ray gently scraped the soil away from the fabric. It was pretty much in shreds from decay over the many years. But surprisingly, it soon became very, very clear that beneath its wrap were what appeared to be the remains of a human skeleton. The group stared intently as Ray's shovel revealed more and more particles of bone matter and finally, a human skull. There was a collective gasp as each person stood motionless with mouths open and a look of shock on their faces. It was a grave. This was all just too unbelievable.

"My God," said Donald. "What in hell is this all about?

Ray's shovel then hit a hard object. It sounded like something metal. He dropped to his knees and began digging with his hands until he uncovered a small metal box. It was a cashbox, like one used in a home or small business operation. It had a small flip latch that held the lid on tight. He handed the box up to RJ. He took it and hesitated for a moment.

"Do you want to open this, Aunt Louise?" he asked.

"No, I'm too shaky. You do it," she told him as she stepped back onto the dock and sat down again.

RJ stooped down next to her. He pulled the latch down and opened the box. Everyone gathered closer for a look. Inside the box was a Mason jar with a tightly sealed lid. And, inside the jar was what appeared to be a note. RJ attempted to open the jar. It took several tries before the lid finally gave way. He unscrewed it, removed the note and put the jar back in the metal box and laid it on the ground. Then he unfolded the note and began to read.

My Dearest Sandra,
What a strange turn of events I have suffered through
these past several hours. My heart is broken. I have
learned your precious secret. Someone left a letter for

200

me on the porch table. At first I thought it was one of your letters. But it wasn't. It revealed every ugly detail. I cannot tell you how hurt I was and especially how angry. I knew you and Eddie were close. It all makes sense now—all those times the two of you spent talking. I just did not know exactly how close...until I read the letter left for me. It told how you and Eddie had made a fool of me. Whoever it was who wrote the letter saw the two of you in the storeroom at your father's store and how you removed each other's clothes and then committed the ultimate offense that has left me reeling in disbelief. How could you? How could Eddie? What a fool I have been. And now, here lies Eddie, the victim of my anger. The hatred and hurt I feel. The revenge I sought. I only meant to confront him but he denied doing anything other than kissing you goodbye. I hit him and told him to tell me the truth. He kept denying it. I kept hitting him. I had no feelings. He's dead. I did not mean to kill him, but it happened anyway. So now, my dear Sandra, I leave you the one you truly wanted...your treasure. I loved you so much and now everything is gone, as I will be too. I do not think I will survive the war. I have no need to. I have no want to. I have lost everything.

R

Louise stood up suddenly. There was a look of horror on her face. Tears were streaming down her cheeks.

"Nooooooo." she screamed in a loud screeching voice.

Then she leaped off the dock and down onto the marshy beach where she ran into the river, screaming blood-curdling sounds of agony. She was totally in shock as she continued deeper into the murky waters of the Alder Branch. She dove under the surface and did not come up for the longest time. By now, RJ and Donald were in quick pursuit, screaming at Louise to stop. When they caught up with her RJ grabbed her hair and pulled her head out of the water. She choked and spit water from her mouth.

"Noooo. Noooo. Leave me be," she yelled at them. "I want to die."

"Aunt Louise," RJ yelled, calm down. Everything will be okay. It's okay. Come back to shore with me."

Louise continued to flail her arms at both RJ and Donald as they attempted to hold her and calm her down. She would have none of it. She broke loose and backed off, deeper into the water. She began pounding her fist, raising them up and down, up and down, beating the surface of the water with all the strength she had.

"It's my fault." she said, "You don't understand. It is all my fault." Her sobs grew even stronger. She scratched her fingers down her cheeks and kept reeling back and forth and up and down in the water. RJ and Donald finally had a tight hold of both her arms and dragged her back toward the shore. She broke loose again and sat in knee-deep water, still repeatedly pounding the surface with her fists; still wailing uncontrollably.

"I did it. I did it," she yelled. "I should die. I must die. I made all this misery. Me, a stupid little teenage girl who just wanted to have him to myself. My God, this is all so unbelievable. What have I done?"

"It's okay, Aunt Louise," RJ kept saying. "Come, let's go in and get dried off. It's cold. None of this is your fault. We are all shocked just like you. But you can't blame yourself for any of this."

Louise remained sitting in the water, now pulling at her hair, still hysterical and out of control.

"No no no no no," she screamed. "I did this. Me! I wrote the letter to Robert. I wanted him. I loved him so much. I was jealous of Sandra, always jealous. I wrote the letter and left it for him on his porch just where she would leave her letters for him. It was all a lie. One big fat lie. I made it all up about Sandra and Eddie. It never happened. Sandra loved Robert more than anything in the world. But I wanted him to leave Sandra so I could have him. So I made the whole story up. I thought if he left her, then when he came home from the war, he would fall in love with me. I did all this. I went to the library and used a typewriter so he would never know who wrote the letter. I loved him so much. I just wanted him to myself. I never imagined all this would happen; how all these lives would be ruined because of me—a stupid jealous little girl who betrayed my dear, dear sister and caused Robert to do that to Eddie and then give up on himself. No no no! I cannot bear all this, this horror I created. Poor Robert, poor Sandra...and poor, poor Eddie. All these lives ruined because of me. These wonderful people I loved lost everything. And I never knew until this moment that it was all my fault. Oh Donald, I am so so sorry you found that letter and had to find out who it was meant for. It should have stayed a dead letter. Death is all it has revealed."

Louise sat waist deep in the water, emotionally drained and exhausted. Donald and RJ slowly pulled her up onto her feet and walked her to shore. It was a numbing moment for everyone and no one there knew quite what to say or what to do.

*****

It would soon be dark along the shoreline of the Alder Branch, just a short distance up from the Corsica River and the great Chesapeake Bay beyond. Another morning and evening had slipped in and then out, just as they had the day before and would again the day after.

Here, year after year, most days seemed pretty much like all the rest as each generation dutifully followed the one before. There was seldom any serious disruption to the pattern; few deviations to the norm. Life on the Eastern Shore was good, wholesome...stable.

Forty years, more or less half a lifetime, had gone by since a young boy sat in a high school math class, the girl of his dreams seated just a short distance to his right. The button on her blouse, the second one down from the top, had come unfastened. There, for the briefest of moments, life was bursting with excitement and adventure...an unusual occurrence for any youngster growing up in the small town of Centreville.

But not until a soldier's letter, mailed that same forty years ago and finally arriving home, would at least one day on Maryland's Eastern Shore never again be like the rest.

Author Note

Reviews, even if just a sentence or two, are critically important to independent authors. If you enjoyed this book, or if you have a comment otherwise, I would greatly appreciate your leaving it on the page for this book at amazon.com.

Simply go to amazon.com and search the title of the book with the author's last name and follow on through to where "Customer Reviews" can be left.

Additional information about my books and access to my blog, are available via http://marckuhn.com

Thank you so much!
Marc Kuhn

ACKNOWLEDGEMENTS

I hope you enjoyed DEAD LETTER. I certainly enjoyed writing it. I did have some help, however. There were folks along the way who set me straight on some facts or offered insight that the book would have otherwise been lacking. I am grateful to all of them and if the book is successful, they should certainly get some credit for making that happen.

Russ Carter lives in Great Falls, Virginia. There, he dabbles in stamp collecting and represents one of those obscure organizations you could never fathom even existed. It's called *The Military Postal History Society*. Russ has an expert's answer for just about every question you can think of regarding how the U.S. military mail system worked during World War II. Needless to say, the time he took to share his knowledge with me is priceless.

Jennifer L. Rhodes works for the Agriculture & Natural Resources Department for Maryland's Queen Anne's County. Jennifer knew all about farming along the Eastern Shore in the 1940s. She made sure I had my crops in a row.

Robert A. Elliot is Commodore of the Corsica River Yacht Club in Centreville. He probably doesn't think he had much to contribute here, but sometimes simply providing a good lead is worth its weight in gold. He hooked me up with Mary Margaret Revell Goodwin. Mary is perhaps the most authoritative historian for the town of Centreville and its surroundings. She set my geography straight and corrected some terminology I was using that would have driven the locals nuts. I hope I have been a worthy student.

The keen eye of Lori Shepard Grasso helped reveal misspellings, misplaced punctuation and other "misfits" in the original manuscript. I am totally inept at seeing my own mistakes. I kept her very busy. Thank you, Lori.

Very lucky me, I have a good friend who has spent a lifetime writing and editing books, news reports and features that appear in the newspaper and on the radio, and I'm sure a bunch of other stuff. He would hate that sentence I just wrote—too long! If this book is good, it is because of him. I put the ideas and the words down...he made them readable. Thank you, Ted Landphair.

Friends and family always come into play when you undertake a project like writing a book. My wife Rosemarie gets her usual gold-plated trophy for having the patience to stop whatever she was doing to listen to me play out a scene in the book and query her reaction. Meanwhile my son, Jeff, went through the manuscript, gave me a helpful critique and corrected one or two historical mistakes he spotted. His watching all those World War II documentaries on cable obviously paid off. And too, a lost old friend, Ron Carmean, recently surfaced just in time to offer a lot of encouragement and a list of improvements I took to heart.

Then there are Toni the cat and Bill the Dog. Toni was a constant companion—albeit a sleeping one—who draped herself atop my printer throughout the writing of the entire book. Bill, on the other hand, was always wide awake and reminding me to take a break from the computer and take him for a walk. Toni and Bill were always there for me in my writing sanctuary and I bounced quite a few ideas off of them. As you might guess, they never bounced back with anything much, but they were there for me nonetheless.

And finally, I thank my mother and father, to whom this book is dedicated. While they both scurried off to an office every day before working couples were the norm, they made sure my brother and I had a great childhood with some special treats along the way. Among them were two summers at a camp on the Eastern Shore of Maryland, on the banks of the Corsica River. Obviously, those two summers are still ripe with wonderful memories of my favorite place on earth…the great Chesapeake Bay.

Marc Kuhn
July 2013